OUTSTANDING AWARDS AND HONORS FOR

Music FOR Tigers

- Honor Book for the Green Earth Book Award
- Honor Book for the OLA Forest of Reading Silver Birch Award
- Finalist for the MYRCA Sundogs Award
- Finalist for the Rocky Mountain Book Award
- Winner of the Northern Lights Book Award
- A White Ravens Selection
- A *Kirkus Reviews* Best Middle Grade Book of the Year
- A USBBY Outstanding International Book
- A *Washington Post Kidspost* Summer Book Club selection
- A Junior Library Guild selection
- A CBC Books Best Canadian YA and Middle-Grade Books of 2020 selection
- A *Quill & Quire* Books of the Year honorable mention
- A CCBC *Best Books for Kids & Teens* selection
- An OLA Best Bet

"Kadarusman masterfully creates a lush, magical world where issues associated with conservation, neurodiversity, and history intersect in surprising and authentic ways.... Crucially, the author acknowledges the original, Indigenous inhabitants of the land as experts...A beautiful conservation story told in a rich setting and peopled with memorable characters."—*Kirkus* ★ **Starred Review**

Music
FOR
Tigers

BY GOVERNOR GENERAL'S AWARD FINALIST
MICHELLE KADARUSMAN

pajamapress

Hardcover edition first published in Canada and the United States in 2020

This edition first published in Canada and the United States in 2021
Text copyright © 2020 Michelle Kadarusman
This edition copyright © 2021 Pajama Press Inc.

10 9 8 7 6 5 4 3 2

 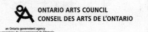

The publisher gratefully acknowledges the support of the Canada Council for the Arts and the Ontario Arts Council for its publishing program. We acknowledge the financial support of the Government of Canada through the Canada Book Fund (CBF) for our publishing activities.

Library and Archives Canada Cataloguing in Publication

Title: Music for tigers / Michelle Kadarusman.
Names: Kadarusman, Michelle, 1969- author.
Description: First edition. | "By Governor General's Award finalist."
Identifiers: Canadiana 2019021810X | ISBN 9781772780543 (hardcover).--9781772781892 (softcover)
Classification: LCC PS8621.A33 M87 2020 | DDC j813/.6—dc23

Publisher Cataloging-in-Publication Data (U.S.)

Names: Kadarusman, Michelle, 1969-, author.
Title: Music for Tigers / Michelle Kadarusman.
Description: Toronto, Ontario Canada : Pajama Press, 2020. | Summary: "Middle-school student Louisa wants to spend the summer practicing violin for a place in the youth symphony, but is instead sent to the Tasmanian rain forest camp of her Australian relatives. There she learns that her family secretly protects the last of the supposedly extinct Tasmanian tigers. When an encroaching mining operation threatens the hidden sanctuary, Louisa realizes her music can help"— Provided by publisher.
Identifiers: ISBN 978-1-77278-054-3 (hardback) | | 978-1-77278-189-2 (paperback)
Subjects: LCSH: Tiger – Tasmania -- Juvenile fiction. | Musicians -- Juvenile fiction. | Endangered species – Juvenile fiction. | BISAC: JUVENILE FICTION / Science & Nature / Environment. | JUVENILE FICTION / People & Places / Australia & Oceania.
Classification: LCC PZ7.K333Mu |DDC [F] – dc23

Cover and book design—Rebecca Bender
Cover Images: **Valentyna Chukhlyebova, Bella Bender, Potapov Alexander, Ratana21/Shutterstock**
Map design—Sarfaraaz Alladin
Author photograph—Micah Ricardo Riedl

Manufactured by Friesens
Printed in Canada

Pajama Press Inc.
11 Davies Ave. Suite 103, Toronto, ON M4M 2A9

Distributed in Canada by UTP Distribution
5201 Dufferin Street Toronto, Ontario Canada, M3H 5T8

Distributed in the U.S. by Ingram Publisher Services
1 Ingram Blvd. La Vergne, TN 37086, USA

For Sophia

The author acknowledges *the Tasmanian Aboriginal community as traditional owners and custodians of all lands in Tasmania and pays respect to Elders past and present.*

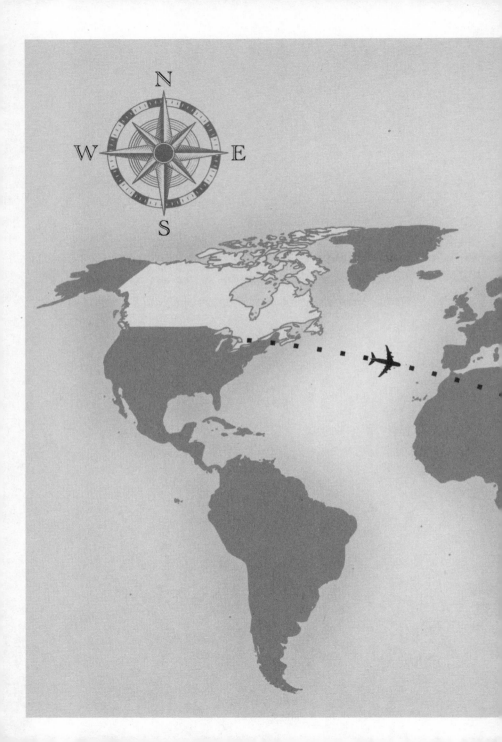

Tasmania

Tarkine
Region

1

Vivaldi and Bunyips

The first sound I hear in the forest at the bottom of the world is Vivaldi's "Spring" from *The Four Seasons*. There's a movement in the violin concerto that's meant to mimic the sound of birds. When I step off the bus in the Tarkine bush, that's exactly what I hear. An orchestra of birdsong descends like musical rain from the Tasmanian treetops as I'm enveloped into a landscape of towering bluish-green eucalypts.

"Listen to that," I say to myself and lift my face toward the swaying gums. The giant trees look exactly the way my sister Sophie described them to me, including their minty pine scent.

My uncle—I know it's my uncle because he's the only

one standing at the bus stop and my mom told me he would be waiting for me; she also told me to expect him to be "a little odd"—tips his wide-brimmed hat to the bus driver, picks up my duffel bag, and tramps toward what barely looks wide enough to be called a path between the trees. My uncle is tall and has a bushy, ginger-colored beard, exactly like the photo my mom had shown me. "Let's go," he calls over his shoulder before disappearing into thick foliage.

My mom had not been wrong about the odd part.

Millie, the bus driver, gives me a thumbs-up, waves, and toots the horn before continuing on her way along the narrow, winding mountain road. Millie had listened patiently to me the whole way from Launceston. She'd heard all about how my parents are spending the summer in the wetlands of southern Ontario so my mom can study an endangered amphibian called the Fowler's toad. About how I was sent here—to my mom's family's bush camp—in the remote Tasmanian rain forest. And how, apparently, the camp is being bulldozed soon so this is my last chance to have "the experience of a lifetime." She also got an earful about the fact that what I really want to be doing this summer is practicing for a place in the Toronto Symphony Youth Orchestra. Preferably in the comfort of my own home.

Millie had nodded politely for the entire four-hour ride.

"I think it's hard for them to believe that I don't want to be a scientist like them," I said. "Believe it or not, I don't want to spend my days knee-deep in swamp water looking for endangered toads like my mother, or traipsing around the globe writing about the environment like my father, or talking to trees like my sister, Sophie." I sighed. "I want to be a violinist."

Millie was an excellent listener. Although, come to think of it, I wonder how much she was able to hear with those earbuds she was wearing. Anyway, she was a lot nicer than my uncle, who I now scamper to catch up with.

"The birds!" I call out once I am within arm's reach of my uncle. "It's Vivaldi's 'Spring'!"

My uncle's large frame keeps walking. I look around me. We're in the middle of nowhere, surrounded by nothing except soaring eucalypts and enormous ground ferns. I grip my violin case and swing my backpack over my shoulder. I hurry to keep up.

"How far do we have to walk?" I ask him, already breathless.

He grunts and swats his hand in a forward motion that I guess means *Just follow*. With no other choice, I do, keeping my eyes glued to the dirt path. I read all about Australian dead-lies on the airplane from Toronto. Practically everything that crawls and slithers is venomous and wants to kill you here—redback spiders, funnel-web spiders, tiger snakes, lowland copperhead snakes, and white-lipped snakes. I'm running the list through my head when I look up and see two black eyes staring back at me.

I scream and stop dead in my tracks.

The beady eyes are attached to a body that looks like a gi-ant rodent with rabbit ears and a long snout. It's peering at me from over my uncle's shoulder.

I scream again and my uncle turns around. "Shhh. You're scaring her," he says.

The critter gives a shrill squeak and hides its furry head in his armpit. I can't help but notice that its orangey-brown fur is the same color as my uncle's beard.

"What...what is it?" I ask. "Is it poisonous?"

"Poisonous?" He chuckles. "Not likely. Are all Canadians so jumpy?"

"Are all Australians so strange?"

"Hm. I'm guessing no." He turns on his bootheel and keeps walking.

Amazing. I'm in the middle of nowhere with a bearded giant and his color-coordinated sidekick.

"Well, thanks to my nature-crazed parents," I say, speaking to his back, "I'm here walking through the land of creepy-crawlies instead"—I pause to catch my breath— "instead of being safe at home practicing for my audition like I should be." I pluck a piece of tree bark out of my hair. "Honestly, I thought it was the grown-ups who were meant to worry about keeping us kids safe, not the other way around."

"You talk a lot," he mumbles from up ahead.

We huff on. And on and on. The only view of his sidekick now is a tuft of white hair at the end of its tail that pokes out from under his arm. I keep my ears tuned, hoping to catch Vivaldi again, but all I hear is my own ragged breath. How many miles have we walked? My backpack begins to feel like a deadweight and I start sweating despite the cool temperature. The sweat brings flies. A flying squadron of fat black pests buzz around my face and dive-bomb my eyes and mouth.

"Stop!" I double over, coughing. "I think I swallowed one." I cough some more. "Yuck!"

My uncle stops. "Don't worry," he says in his deadpan voice. "It won't kill you."

I stand up and take the canteen of water he hands me. "Are you sure?" I ask.

"That, on the other hand," he says, pointing his chin over my left shoulder, "that might."

I spin around. "What? Where?"

"You didn't see it?" he asks.

"Where?" I keep spinning, frantically scanning the dense green foliage around me. "What is it?"

"A bunyip." He sets down my duffel bag and scratches his beard. "They're pretty bad around here."

"A bunyip?" I don't remember reading about bunyips in my guidebook on Australian deadlies. "What's a bunyip?"

He nods gravely while I swat and pat my head, up and down my jeans, and all over my hoodie to make sure nothing is crawling on me.

"Is it a kind of spider?" I ask. "Get it off me!"

"You haven't heard about the famous Australian bunyip?" he asks with a twinkle. "It has fur and feathers and a tail and claws and a beak. It bounces like a kangaroo and laughs like a kookaburra before it eats you up in a single gulp, like a great white shark."

I stop spinning and swatting. "Oh. I get it. You're *joking*." I sigh. "Very funny."

My uncle has a full-belly kind of laugh, he puts his whole body into it. "It gets them every time," he says, slapping his thigh.

"Oh brother, it's going to be a long summer," I say.

"Kid, it's not summer here," he says. "You're in the southern hemisphere now. It's winter."

"Lucky me," I say.

"Look on the bright side," he says, stroking the ball of fur that is now curled up in the crook of his arm. "You've got me, my excellent jokes, and Piggy here to keep you company."

"Is that his name?" I watch as the critter pokes the air with his long snout, making sniffling noises in my direction. "What kind of animal is he?"

"Her. Female," he says, still not answering my question. He takes back the canteen and picks up my bag again, swinging it over his shoulder. "Come on. Not much farther."

We keep walking but at a slower pace. After a few minutes I hear the Vivaldi birdsong again.

"Do you hear that?" I pause to listen. "I finally get what Vivaldi's 'Spring' concerto was meant to sound like. It's so beautiful."

"That's just the currawongs," he says, looking to the treetops before taking another step. "C'mon, kid," he calls. "Better get a move on before that bunyip gets you."

I suspect, among his many strange personality traits, my uncle is tone-deaf.

2

Camp Nowhere

We finally come to the end of the trail.

"Welcome to paradise." My uncle opens his arms to the sky as we walk into a dusty clearing at the end of the dirt path. Piggy clings to his shoulder, trembling. Several small, crumbling cabins squat in a semicircle facing a wide river. I scan the camp. I can understand why it's being demolished, most of the buildings look half-collapsed already. It sure doesn't look like paradise.

I spy a mud-caked jeep parked at the end of a dirt road.

"Wait. So we could have driven here?" I ask.

"Of course," he replies. "How do you think I get to the pub?"

I stare at him, blinking and swatting flies that will not stop buzzing around my face.

"Sorry." He clears his throat. "I should have introduced myself properly at the bus stop. It's just that Piggy here, she is shy of strangers and she doesn't like the car, so…"

"So we walked," I say.

"So we walked," he agrees. "We do a lot of that around here. I'm your uncle Rufus." He holds out his hand. "Uncle Ruff for short. Or just call me Ruff like everyone else does. Pleased to meet you."

"I'm Louisa." His large hand is calloused but warm. "Everyone calls me Lou but I prefer Louisa," I say.

"Gotcha," he replies.

I look around at the camp. The birdsong of the bush and the rush of the river are starkly different from the city noise and traffic sounds where I live in downtown Toronto.

"Besides, your mum said you need some good old fresh air and exercise." Uncle Ruff has started to walk toward one of the buildings.

"That sounds like my mom all right," I say, following him.

"Come on, I'll get Piggy settled and then I'll show you to your digs."

We walk up some creaky stairs to a small weather-beaten clapboard cabin and then through a screen door that screeches loudly as it opens before banging closed again. I look around the screened-in porch. An old armchair sits in one corner with empty beer cans on the floor beside it. The porch smells musty and smoky. A transistor radio is perched on the window ledge.

At the other end of the porch is a makeshift animal pen. Uncle Ruff places Piggy gently inside and she scrambles underneath a branch. The pen is filled with bark, leaves, and gum branches.

"Is she a pet?" I ask.

"Yes and no. Sort of. She's a pig-footed bandicoot. They are, um…" He coughs. "Rare. And she's old. And sick. The pen keeps her safe from predators." He checks the water bowl before collecting the empty beer cans. He looks at me and winks. "The maid didn't show up this morning."

"Let me guess," I say, following him inside the cabin. "She was eaten by a bunyip."

Uncle Ruff gives a chuckle as he puts the cans in the garbage can. "Kid, we just might be related after all."

I notice that behind his beard, Ruff's smile is the same as my mom's. He fills a woodstove with small round logs. The cabin is cozy with timber walls and an old Persian rug on the wooden floor. The main room includes a small kitchen. I notice a door leading from the kitchen which I guess is Uncle Ruff's bedroom.

"My mom said the camp is being demolished soon," I say.

"Yep. All in the name of *progress*," he says in a mocking tone. "It's all gonna be bulldozed," he goes on, more seriously. "To make an access road and a bridge over the river. For the local tin and iron ore mines."

I notice a laptop computer sitting on the kitchen table.

"Can I go online? I want to let my parents know I'm here."

"Afraid not. No Internet here." He continues to arrange logs in the stove. "But we can go next door to the Eco Lodge. Theirs works pretty good most of the time."

I check my watch. It's the middle of the night at home and I'm not even sure if Mom and Dad are in cell range where they are in the Southern Ontario wetlands. I bite my lip wondering what to do. I know my parents will be worried. I've been traveling for over twenty-four hours.

"Don't worry, Lou. I spoke with your mum when you landed in Launceston and made the transfer to the bus." He stands up and taps his nose. "I have my spies."

"It's Louisa," I remind him. "And you did? Thank you."

"Hungry?" Uncle Ruff is opening and closing cabinets in search of food.

"Starving," I say. "The food wasn't great on the airplane."

I dust off a kitchen stool and gingerly sit myself down at the counter of the small kitchenette. Uncle Ruff has moved to the fridge and is standing with the door open, shaking his head. He closes the fridge finally and eyeballs the last unopened cupboard.

"Aha!" he says, victoriously holding a package high above his head. "Prepare for the best Cup-a-Soup you've ever had in your life."

After I eat an underwhelming mug of watery soup Uncle Ruff leads me to my cabin. It's smaller than Uncle Ruff's and without a screened porch. He shoulders the old wooden door a few times before it creaks open. "Yep," he says, peering around. "Exactly how she left it."

"Who?" I ask.

"Your sister. I thought you'd like to have her cabin. She made it up real nice when she was here. See? She even put up curtains." I look at a faded piece of cotton with frayed edges hanging over the grimy glass.

"This is where Sophie stayed?" I ask.

"Yep," he confirms.

"But that was years ago," I say. "She's in university now."

"Time flies!" says Uncle Ruff. "Make yourself at home. I'll bring your stuff over later."

The cabin is about the size of our garden shed at home. Strings of cobwebs hang from the corners of the ceiling. "Are there spiders in here?" I ask.

"Nah," says Uncle Ruff unconvincingly. "Not likely."

I step inside hesitantly and look around as Uncle Ruff tramps off. A metal-framed single bed takes up most of the space. An ancient-looking dining chair doubles as a nightstand with a few books stacked on top. I sit on the bed. The frame squeaks and the mattress releases a puff of dust. A thick layer of grime covers every surface. I glance at the spines of the books on the chair. *The Ancient Huon Pine*, *The Tarkine*, *Shadow of the Forest*. They are exactly the kind of books Sophie likes to read. I think of my big sister and feel a stab of homesickness. If Sophie were here she would give me one of her lopsided smiles and tell me to quit being a princess. It's true. I would kill for a hot shower and a plate of Mom's roast chicken. I think longingly of my soft, carpeted bedroom with its crisp sheets, lavender-scented pillows, and fluffy duvet.

How am I supposed to get through six entire weeks of this? Six weeks of an odd relative with a strange pet, instant soup, and a filthy cabin? I reach for my violin case and do what I always do. I forget everything else and start to play. My fingers feel stiff and awkward as I move through the musical scales. I'm more tired from the journey than I realized.

The next thing I know, I'm waking up to the most awful smell.

I must have fallen asleep. Jet làg. I look around to get my bearings; it takes a while for my eyes to adjust to the inky darkness. Someone, Uncle Ruff, I guess, has put a heavy quilt on top of me. I see he has set my bags next to the bed. But there is no accounting for that smell. It's so pungent, I can almost taste it. It reminds me of skunk but worse.

Then I hear a strange, high-pitched noise...*cough, cough, yip, yip*. An animal sound I've never heard before. I snuggle into the quilt, shut my eyes, and breathe through my mouth, hoping to fall back to sleep. One thing is for sure: I am not about to venture into the spooky nighttime wilderness to find out what belongs to that stink.

3

Devil Tracks

In the morning, after a bowl of stale cornflakes, Uncle Ruff says we'll go to the Eco Lodge so I can e-mail home. He is worried about Piggy. She isn't doing great, he says. Her breath is labored and she didn't eat her breakfast. "We'll leave her here," he says. "The drive will be too much for her." He leans into her pen and pets her gently before we walk to the jeep.

"I thought you said the Eco Lodge was just next door," I say as I climb into Uncle Ruff's car.

"Next door in the bush is different to next door in the city," he says as the old jeep splutters to life.

He isn't kidding. The drive takes forty-five minutes over winding gravel roads.

"You should have seen how bad it used to be before the road was leveled," Uncle Ruff says as I'm flung around in my seat. I can barely imagine how it could be any worse. I cling tightly to the jeep's hand strap.

"I woke up to a funny smell last night," I tell Uncle Ruff as we bounce along. "It was awful, kind of like skunk, but not skunk. Really gross."

Uncle Ruff scratches his beard but doesn't speak.

"Do you know what it was?" I prompt.

"Maybe." But he doesn't offer what that might be. "Look," he says instead. "Here we are."

We turn into a paved drive. A sign reads:

THE NORTHWEST ECO LODGE: BETWEEN RIVER AND SKY

As we get out of the jeep a small group of people, most with cameras around their necks and wearing hiking boots, are standing in the parking lot. A woman is speaking to them. She wears a wide-brimmed hat and stands tall with authority.

"Welcome to the Tarkine," she says, "traditional land of the northwest tribe of Indigenous Tasmanians. The Aboriginal name for the area is *takayna*, all lowercase. For an estimated thirty-five thousand years, until late in the nineteenth century, the Tarkine was home to the Tarkiner people. European settlers forced the Aboriginal population from their lands all over Tasmania, including here in the Tarkine. Today's Aboriginal community, descendants of the first Tasmanians, are the true custodians of all the land."

The tourists in the parking lot nod solemnly, their gaze fixed on the woman who is speaking. Uncle Ruff and I stand together and listen too.

"The Tarkine is one of the largest temperate rain forests on earth," she continues. "This vast tract of wilderness includes wild rivers, coastal headlands, button grass plains, ancient Huon pines, giant eucalypts, and vertical ferns. It is home to abundant birdlife and wildlife such as quolls, devils, black swans, wallabies, pademelon, wombats, possums, platypuses, and the endangered Tasmanian wedge-tailed eagle." She pauses and surveys her audience. "But, devastatingly, it is all under threat from human industry that imperils its survival. Only a small area of the Tarkine is designated as a national park and protected. Logging and mining are a real and continued threat in the region. Bulldozers destroy thousands of years of complex biodiversity in an instant. Here at the Northwest Eco Lodge our mission is to provide low-impact eco-tourism to demonstrate that the region can generate an environmentally safe source of revenue, one that respects and preserves this unique and ir-replaceable rain forest." She clasps her hands together at her chest. "Old growth forests help combat climate change. In our current climate crisis, protecting them is imperative."

The tourists clap and crowd around the woman, peppering her with questions.

"That's my mum."

I turn to see who has spoken loudly in my ear. A boy around my age is standing very close. He has large eyes and feathery brown bangs that make me think of a barn owl I saw on a television nature program. His eyes dart around my face before settling somewhere above my head.

"I'm Colin," he says. He taps his right temple with his fingertips as he speaks. "Do you want to see some devil tracks?"

I take a step back. "What are devil tracks?" I ask.

"If you come with me I can show you."

"No, wait," I say. "I need to send an e-mail, I'm here with my uncle—"

Uncle Ruff slaps Colin on the back. "G'day mate," he says. "This is my niece, Lou."

"Louisa," I correct him.

"Right, Louisa," says Uncle Ruff. "She's come all the way from Canada."

Colin looks unimpressed. He continues to tap his temple. "I know who she is," he says. "Mum told me you were coming today for the Internet."

"Go on and look at the tracks first," Uncle Ruff says to me. "Meet me back here. Mel will be finished with the hikers and we can use the computer."

Colin leads the way past the group of hikers to the edge of the parking lot and toward the river. I follow him along the sandy river's edge for a few minutes.

"Look here," says Colin. He squats down and peers at the sand on the riverbank. "You see? Here." His finger follows a trail of small footprints in the damp sand. "They're devil tracks."

"What exactly is a devil?" I ask, bending down to take a look. The tracks are perfectly formed—round pads with four claws, larger than a cat's but smaller than an average dog's.

"To be accurate, a Tasmanian devil," says Colin. "Distant relative of the Tasmanian tiger. Tasmanian tigers are thought to be extinct." Colin stares at me with his large eyes, studying my reaction. I tilt my head, not sure what he's hoping I'll say. "Tasmanian devils are carnivorous marsupials," he goes on, looking back down at the tracks. "About the size of a Jack Russell terrier. They are known for being bad tempered—screeching and snarling when they feed and muck about. The population in this area is healthy. That's good. There's a facial disease that's causing them to become endangered." He stands up, still gazing at the tracks. "They like to play tricks too. There's been one around the Eco Lodge stealing shoes. That's why I came to the river to have a look. Sometimes they hunt frogs and tadpoles down here."

"Stealing shoes?" I ask.

"Yes. Who knows why." Colin speaks in a monotone voice so I'm not sure if he's joking or serious. "Like I said, they like to muck about. Little tricksters."

I look out over the river. The water is breathlessly still and it reflects the pastel-blue sky and billowy clouds like a mirror. I hear the single cry of a bird. Maybe it's one of the wedge-tailed eagles that Colin's mom mentioned.

"What's that over there?" I ask, pointing to a landmass in the middle of the wide river. A sand-colored cliff looms high above the tree line. "I can see it from our camp as well."

"You don't know?" he asks.

I shake my head. "No."

"That's Convict Rock," he says. "People say it's haunted."

I raise my eyebrows. "Haunted?"

"That's what people say, but really it's a long skinny island with nothing on it except rocks and caves. There's an old story about escaped convicts hiding there. Did you know that Tasmania was a convict colony?" he asks.

I nod. This much at least, I do know.

"To be accurate, the British settled the island as a penal colony in 1803," he says. "It was notoriously brutal. They called it Van Diemen's Land then." Colin glances at me before continuing. "So the story goes that two escaped convicts hid over on Convict Rock and they starved to death. People say their spirits still haunt the rock." He gestures at the river. "It stops the tourists from going there."

I watch the milk-white belly of an eagle as it circles silently above the rocky cliffs on Convict Rock.

"I'm going back," he announces. "Mum will have finished her talk by now." He walks toward the Eco Lodge. "The hikers will have set out on the trails." I notice he has stopped tapping his temple. "Did you know I have a five-star rating on TripAdvisor as a bushwalking guide?" he asks.

I shake my head no.

"It's true," he says. "To be accurate, I have forty-three five-star ratings. There are twelve different walking trails available from the Eco Lodge and I have memorized each one. The distance in kilometres, the level of hiking difficulty, and the various opportunities to observe flora and fauna."

"Um...that's cool."

He turns and steps purposefully back along the riverbank, and I follow. As we make our way through the parking lot, what look like miniature kangaroos hop about here and there, sniffing the ground and chewing. They don't seem the least bit timid. One blinks at us expectantly as we pass by.

"Pademelon," says Colin. "The name *pademelon* is Aboriginal. They are also sometimes referred to as the rufous wallaby. They are some of the smallest of the macropod marsupials, the family of marsupials including the kangaroo, wallaby, wallaroo, and so on. The hikers feed them even though they're not meant to."

"They're so cute," I say, watching as they eventually hop out of the parking lot and into the bush. "You really know a lot about the bush and the animals," I add.

"Sometimes I get nervous speaking to kids I don't know," he says, abruptly changing the topic. Colin has a directness that takes me off guard. I search for what to say.

"You don't seem nervous," I answer finally.

"Well, you're different," he says.

"Different how?" I ask.

"You sound funny," he says. "Your accent. You don't sound like any of the kids at my school."

We've reached Uncle Ruff and Colin's mum who are standing at the base of the stairs leading to the Eco Lodge reception area. Colin's mom puts out her hand for me to shake.

"I'm Mel," she says. "Pleased to meet you." She turns to Colin and then to me again with a look of apology. "Sorry if it sounds like my son is insulting you." She looks at Colin, her brow creased. "You've heard all kinds of accents at the Eco Lodge, Colin. Why would you call Louisa's funny?"

"Funny in a good way," says Colin, looking skyward. "It sounds like she could never say any of the mean things."

Mel gives her son a sad smile. "And I'm sure she wouldn't," she says quietly.

Colin bounds up the steps and Mel gestures for us to follow her into the Eco Lodge reception area. Colin disappears though a door without saying another word.

"He likes you, Louisa," says Mel with a grin as she watches the door swing closed. "Come on, I'll show you where you can get online." Mel cocks her head and adds: "We meet at last. And don't you look the spitting image of your mum!" She throws her arms around me.

4

Eleanor's Tiger

On the way back to the camp, I ask Uncle Ruff about the strange odor again, from the night before.

"There are two local animals I know that give off a strange scent when they're distressed. One is the Tasmanian devil and the other is the thylacine, best known as the Tasmanian tiger."

"Colin told me about the Tasmanian tiger. He said they're extinct, so it must have been a Tasmanian devil. Colin showed me a devil's tracks on the riverbank. He said the devils like to hunt frogs and tadpoles. Our camp is on the same river, isn't it? Because we can see Convict Rock from our camp as well." I think for a minute. "So it must have been devils, right?"

"He told you about Convict Rock?" Uncle Ruff asks.

I nod, distracted, thinking back to what Colin had actually said. "Colin said Tasmanian tigers are *thought to be* extinct. What does that mean? They *are* extinct, aren't they?"

Uncle Ruff keeps his eyes on the road.

"Let's get back and see how Piggy's doing," he says, yet again dodging my questions.

Piggy is weak and hardly breathing when we arrive back at the camp. Uncle Ruff cradles her in his arms.

"Why don't you take her to a vet?" I ask him.

"It's complicated," he says, his gaze still on Piggy. "Besides, I'm more than qualified to take care of her." He strokes her head gently. "I'm going to try giving her some water with an eyedropper. She looks dehydrated."

I get to work putting away the canned and packaged food items that Mel sent back with us. "I'll be over later to help you get settled in," she had told me. "I'm guessing Ruff hasn't cleaned the place in years."

I open a can of tomato soup and put it on the stove to heat while Uncle Ruff administers single drops of water carefully into Piggy's mouth. I can't help but think of a mother bird feeding her chick. Uncle Ruff is as far from a mother bird as you can imagine, though. He looks more like a large bear.

Once the soup is ready, Uncle Ruff puts Piggy back into her enclosure. She has pepped up a bit after the water. Her snout even sniffs toward the smell of the hot soup.

"What exactly has your mum told you about what we do here?" Uncle Ruff asks as he sits down at the kitchen table.

"I know that she spent her summers here with you and your grandmother," I say, setting down a bowl of soup for each of us.

"Your mum promised she would fill you in before you came here," he says, looking at me with a searching expression. "Are you sure she didn't tell you anything?" he asks again. "What about Sophie?"

I think back to my mom trying multiple times to engage me in conversation before I left, and me telling her over and over again that I didn't have time, that I needed to practice. I remember Sophie wanting to Facetime with me too, and me not having time for that either. I was trying to master my vibrato. I was sure if I could just get my fingerwork right it would be the key to conquering my audition.

"Hm. Maybe they tried," I admit. "I've been kind of... distracted."

I realize with a start that I haven't practiced at all today. I spoon the soup faster into my mouth, wanting to get back to my cabin and get started.

"That's too bad," he says. "It would have been easier if you'd known."

"Known what?" I ask.

"About Piggy, about the camp, about the..." He slurps a spoonful of soup, seemingly stuck for words.

"Does it have something to do with the smell last night?" I prompt.

Uncle Ruff stops eating. He stares at me for a moment and then gets up and goes to his bedroom. He brings back a large plastic folder.

"Piggy is a pig-footed bandicoot," he says, placing the folder on the table. "Not to be confused with the southern brown bandicoot that is found here in Tasmania. The pig-footed bandis were found in arid areas of mainland Australia mostly. It's their feet that made them different, you see. They had front feet like the hooves of a pig or a deer. The hind feet had a fourth toe and a claw like a tiny horse's hoof."

"Wait," I said. "You keep saying *had*. She's still right here, isn't she, with her funny feet?"

He sits back in his chair. "If we could get online, you'd google and find out in a few seconds that pig-footed bandicoots are extinct. Have been since the 1950s."

"But Piggy's right there in her enclosure," I say, gesturing toward the porch.

"Piggy is a descendant of some pig-footed bandicoots that were given to your great-grandmother Eleanor in the 1940s. She started a breeding program with southern brown bandicoots. It had some success early on, but not so much in the past decade or so. Piggy is the last one."

I open my mouth to speak but close it again.

Uncle Ruff holds up his hand. "I know. You have questions. But there's a lot more to the story and Piggy isn't even the beginning. It starts with Shadow."

"Was Shadow one of the first bandicoots?" I ask.

"No," he replies. "Shadow was Eleanor's first tiger."

Tiger. *As in Tasmanian tiger?* Somewhere in the back of my mind something clicks. Snatches of background conversations between Mom and Sophie, and my dad too. Books around the house

34

about animal extinction and an article my dad wrote for an international nature journal about thylacines, or Tasmanian tigers as they're more popularly known. I had just never been interested enough to tune in, my mind was always filled with the violin.

"I can tell you the facts," Uncle Ruff says. "But it's important you know the heart of the place first." He slides the plastic folder across the table to me. "To understand this place, what it's all about, better to hear it from the source," says Uncle Ruff.

I pick up the folder. "The source?" I ask.

"Your great-grandmother Eleanor. That's her journal. What's left of them anyway, after the fire. We almost lost the entire camp in a bushfire, back in the late nineties."

I open the folder and pull out a crumbling journal. Uncle Ruff is right, it barely holds together and only a thin clutch of pages remain.

"Be gentle with it. There's a photocopy of the journal pages in there as well. Best to read from those instead."

I close the musty old book and flip through the photocopied pages.

Uncle Ruff returns to his bowl of soup. "It's time you met Great-Granny Eleanor," he says with a wink.

I finish up my soup and carry the plastic folder back to my cabin and place it on the bed, reaching for my violin.

Great-Granny will have to wait, violin comes first. Always.

I take the books off the old chair and sit down.

I straighten my back and shoulders, remembering the words drilled into me by my violin teacher, Ms. Ling: *We play from our posture first!*

I spread out my sheet music on the bed, pick up my instrument, and settle into the chin rest. I feel the familiar comfort of the bow in my hand and begin to play. The acoustics of the cabin are good. All the hard surfaces allow me to hear every bad note I play. Maybe it's jet lag, maybe it's from being in the opposite hemisphere, but I know I sound awful.

Sharper! Flatter! Slower! I hear Ms. Ling shouting above my terrible bow changes. *Intonation! Faster! Smoother!*

A sense of panic builds inside me. I have to *practice, practice, practice.* Not just for the mental discipline but for the physical strength needed for a full performance. By the time I go back home I have to be good enough to audition again for a place with the Toronto Symphony Youth Orchestra. Better than good enough—I have to be perfect. Everything else has to come second to practicing. I don't care if I've been sent to the end of the world, to the middle of nowhere, with all kinds of strange wildlife happenings, I am not going to let go of my dream.

I lift my bow to begin again but spot something that makes my heart stop.

5

Bush Law

A spider the size of a man's hand is crawling slowly along the top of the doorframe. Its milk-chocolate-colored body is hairy and easily the size of a chicken egg. I'm too scared to scream at first. I watch as it makes its way carefully from the doorframe to the corner of the cabin. Then it settles, crouches, and glares at me. I am positive it plans to pounce. I let out an earsplitting scream.

Uncle Ruff bursts through the door. "What?" he yells. "What is it Lou? Are you okay?"

I shake my head and point above his head. "Be—be careful!" I stammer finally. "It's right behind you!"

Uncle Ruff turns. "What? Where?"

"The spider!" I scream. "In the corner! Can't you see it? It's huge!"

He snorts. "The huntsman, you mean?" He angles his head to get a better look at it. "She's a beauty."

"Please," I beg. "Please kill it."

"Kill it? Nah. We don't kill huntsmen. They eat the bugs, we like them. She's just come inside for a rest. Must be going to rain soon. They usually come in before the rain." He croons at her. "She's a decent size, I'll give you that." He grins. "This girl isn't going to hurt you."

"I don't care. Please get her out." I sob. "Please."

"Okay, kid," he says, reaching for my violin bow. "Hold your horses, no need to fret."

I watch, morbidly fascinated, as he nudges and coaxes the spider onto the end of my bow. Once it grips the bow with its disgustingly long, hairy legs, he opens the door and carries it to some nearby bushes. "Off you go," he tells it. "Lou isn't too keen on your visit, thanks anyway." He pops his head back into the cabin. "You okay now, kid?" He can't keep the smile from his face.

I nod, relief flooding through me as we hear the sound of car tires crunching on the gravel driveway outside. I peek over Uncle Ruff's shoulder to see an SUV with the Eco Lodge logo on the side pull up.

"Come on," he says, offering me his hand. "You've had a scare, you'll be all right. Let's go see Mel." He helps me up and slaps my back playfully. "Look on the bright side. Now you've had your first spider encounter, you're a true-blue Aussie!"

Mel has climbed out of the dusty SUV and is unloading a hamper and a laundry basket from the back seat. The baskets hold promise of food other than canned soup.

"Let me give you a hand," Uncle Ruff tells her.

"Thanks," she says, handing him a basket. "Take this inside, most of it needs to go in the fridge."

"You look as white as a ghost," she says, to me.

"I just saw the biggest spider I have ever seen in my life."

"Huntsman?" Mel looks up at the sky. "Must be going to rain," she says nonchalantly. "Here," she says, handing me a hamper. "The cavalry has arrived."

We go into Uncle Ruff's cabin to unload the baskets. He glances up briefly from where he's now sitting at the kitchen counter, tapping away at his computer.

Mel shakes her head as she looks around the kitchen. "Honestly, Ruff. You may not mind living like a hermit, but I promised your sister I would make sure her daughter doesn't exist on instant noodles for the entire time she's here."

I feel a sudden loneliness at the mention my mom. This place feels so far removed from her; it's hard to remember this is where she's from. Uncle Ruff and Mom grew up in Devonport, a town a couple of hours north of the camp, but they spent their summers here.

"Do you know my mom well?" I ask Mel.

"Yep," says Mel. "Used to, anyways. Your mum was a few years ahead of me at school." Mel throws a package of paper towels at Uncle Ruff and it ricochets off his head. "It was my bad luck to be stuck in the same school year with your uncle." Mel grins at me as Uncle Ruff wordlessly puts the paper towels on the table in front of his computer. He still hasn't taken his eyes off the screen. "Your mum took pity on me." Mel gives me a wink. "But sure, your mum is a good friend. Always will be." She puts her hand on her hip. "Even if she did go and marry a Canadian."

I smile. I like her.

Mel continues to stack food in the fridge. "She e-mailed me a few weeks ago, your mum, and told me about your visit. I promised I'd look out for you."

"She did?" I ask. "That's nice, thank you."

"She sounded pretty jazzed about her fieldwork over there with the amphibian," says Mel. "What's it called again?"

"Fowler's toad."

"Right. That's it," she says, nodding. "And her research position at the university seems really rewarding. It sounds like she's on the brink of some exciting work."

"Could be exciting work for her here too," mumbles Uncle Ruff.

Mel shoots him a look of warning, making me think there's something between Mom and Uncle Ruff that I don't know about.

"I suppose she feels her highly competent veterinarian brother has things under control," says Mel pointedly.

A shadow falls over Uncle Ruff's face. Mel notices it too.

"How is Piggy?" Mel asks.

Uncle Ruff raises his eyebrows and shakes his head. Mel walks out to the porch and bends down to Piggy's pen. She pets her gently. "Good old girl," Mel says in a soothing voice. "We know you need to go soon." She sighs. "Doesn't make it any easier for your dad though."

She looks through the open door to me. "Has he told you about your great-granny yet?"

"No. Well, kind of," I answer. "Apparently I have to read her journal."

"You haven't read them yet?" asks Uncle Ruff, finally looking up from his computer.

I shrug. "I had to practice."

"Oh right," says Mel coming back inside. "Your mum told me you're crazy about the violin."

"I think she'd prefer I were crazy about toads instead," I say.

"I'm not so sure about that," says Mel. "She sounds pretty proud of you. Of both you and your sister." I like the way Mel talks to me like I'm a grown-up. "Come on, she says. "Let's de-spiderize your digs."

We go to my cabin and Mel heads inside with a broom while I wait outside. "Spider free!" she declares after a minute or two. "Come on."

I tentatively peek inside and when I'm satisfied that Mel is right, we get to work cleaning out the cabin. We strip the bed, dust the surfaces, and sweep the floor, then we fill a bucket with soapy water and mop the old floorboards. Mel even insists we take the mattress outside and pound it with the brooms to release more dust. Once we get the mattress back inside and the floorboards are dry, Mel hands me some fresh linens to put on the bed.

"There," she says once a clean quilt has been placed on top. "Much better."

"It really is," I say, sitting on the bed and checking for spiders again. "Thank you."

"Don't worry about the huntsman spiders," Mel tells me. "They're very timid and won't hurt you."

"If you say so," I say hesitantly.

"Truly. And you'll eat the lasagne Colin cooked for dinner tonight," she says. "It's in the oven ready to heat up. And there's salad fixings in the fridge."

"It's really nice of you to bring all of the food and everything," I say. "And Colin cooked? Wow, thanks."

"Out here in the bush we take care of each other," says Mel. "It's the law." She laughs.

We smile at each other.

"Listen, Louisa," she says, "speaking of favors...I have something to ask you."

"Sure, of course," I say.

Mel sits next to me on the bed. "You met Colin today, my son."

"Sure. He showed me some devil tracks," I say.

"You might have noticed that he communicates in a certain way? Quite directly and abruptly? Maybe he was speaking in a loud voice?"

"Um, yeah. I guess a little. He told me about Tasmanian devils and pademelon."

"Right. He's ASD. Autism spectrum disorder. In simpler terms, it means his brain is wired a bit differently. Do you know anyone with ASD?"

"No, but my class participated in World Autism Awareness Day last year so I know a little bit."

"That's great to hear. Okay, so you might know that autism is very different for each person. For Colin, he has challenges with social interactions, reading nonverbal cues and so on." She pauses. "It means making friends has been difficult since he started year seven." Mel looks at me, her eyes soft. "I was hoping, since he seemed so at ease with you, that maybe you wouldn't mind if he came here to stay for part of his school term break. He has two weeks off, starting tomorrow. He often bunks out here with Ruff for his school holidays."

The idea startles me. I'm not exactly the easygoing type when it comes to making friends either. I have two close friends, Remi and Alicia, who also play violin, but we spend most of our time practicing together. We're not the social, gossipy, sleepover types.

"Oh, no, I don't think that will work...I have to practice a lot while I'm here. I have a big audition when I get back to Toronto. I really don't think I'll have time to—to—"

"It will be good, you'll see. Colin will be able to tell you a lot about the history of the area. He is extremely knowledgeable." She grins. "His bushwalking tours are famous on TripAdvisor! Plus, you'll eat well. Cooking is his thing." Mel pats my knee.

"Don't worry, Ruff knows all Colin's quirks, he'll keep him in line." She gets up to leave. The question seems to have been decided. Mel turns as she leaves the cabin. "Thank you," she says. "I am grateful, Louisa. Truly I am."

Oh brother, I think as Mel's SUV motors down the gravel drive, what have I just signed up for? This vacation is getting stranger by the day. Uninvited campers. Extinct bandicoots that aren't extinct after all. Scary-looking spiders that I'm not supposed to be scared of. Odd noises and strange smells in the night. And what exactly is the real story with the Tasmanian tigers?

I guess the only way I'm going to find out is by reading the journal.

6

Eleanor's Journal
Part One

The sky is dimming so I ignite the kerosene lamp the way
Mel had shown me and place it on the chair to give me enough
light to read. The only cabin with a generator for electricity is
Uncle Ruff's.

The folder has *1939* written across it in felt-tip marker. I sit
on the bed and open it. The charred remains of the journal give
off a bitter smoky smell. I gently open the journal; the pages are
almost translucent and the handwriting barely legible in places.
I set the journal aside and lift out the photocopied pages.

Here goes, I say to myself as I lie back on the newly fluffed
pillow. *Time to meet Great-Granny.*

The journal of Eleanor Dover of Burnie, Tasmania

4 January 1939

Mother says I mustn't complain because to do so is for naught and besides an upright piano has no place in the bush. Fiddlesticks! In any case, Father would never waste the horses to cart it here from Burnie.

It pains me greatly to think of my piano alone collecting dust in Grandmother's house with not a soul to play her or keep her tuned! Mother says we will go home to visit at Easter when the piners will take a break from the logging and the camp is empty. Until then I must make do with the trees and the birds for company and mind that I don't daydream so much that I fall behind on my chores.

Grandmother did her best to plead for me to stay behind in Burnie and continue my studies but mother would not have it. Times are too hard not to pitch in and help, Mother said.

Apparently, it will do me *a world of good* to learn practical work instead of the useless lessons that mother learned as a girl. What use are French and cross-stitch when clothes need scrubbing, floors need mopping, dinner needs cooking, and with no money to hire a maid, she says. Grandmother mumbles, "It's enough that her daughter married rough, she need not live hard as well."

Honestly, the two of them never stop their bickering. At least here in the bush I am spared that much.

But Easter is such a long while! I shall go mad with the boredom and without my music to liven my spirits. Mother says my head is filled with nonsense and that I'd do better to worry on my chores instead. Chores, chores, chores! My day is filled with them, collecting eggs, peeling potatoes, cutting carrots, washing the plates, sweeping and scrubbing the cabins. If I ever thought maths and grammar were hard work, I've changed my tune.

The piners are a rough lot and they don't mind making a mess, I can tell you. Mud over every floorboard until mother tacked notices outside the cabins and the food hall that said: DIRTY BOOTS WILL NOT BE FED. We all got a chuckle from it but darned if it did not do the trick. It gives me a smile to see the rough men sitting at the dining table in their socks as I pass the mashed potatoes down the line.

Piners work up a fierce appetite, felling, hauling, and floating the giant eucalypts and the great Huon pine downriver to the mills. No man will risk being left hungry after a day working for the "green gold" as they call the Huon pine. It is backbreaking work, to be sure. As camp foreman, Father does not climb like the piners, but he knows how it goes all right. He did his share of logging before he met Mother. I fancy if this weren't the case the men would not behave as respectfully as they do to Father, and in turn to Mother and me as well.

I try to remind myself how lucky we are to have Father in

a secure job after the long years of the Great Depression. But now it's 1939 and everyone says things are on the up and up for Burnie because of the pulp mill, and the pulp mill needs logs for paper. That means work for Father, and Mother less worried sick all the time.

I promise I am doing my best and trying my very hardest to do my part and not complain, but I think in these pages I am allowed to say it...that I miss my piano very badly.

11 January 1939

Last night I helped Mother darn the piners' socks while Father read the newspaper. We sat around the kitchen table, as we do most evenings. I detest darning but Mother had such a pile of them I knew if I didn't help, she would be up half the night. The piners are forever wearing holes in their socks.

"The trouble in Europe is getting worse," Father muttered, shaking the newspaper. "Talk of another war."

A piner had come up from Burnie and brought last week's *Tasmanian Chronicle*. We are starved for news in the bush. Getting a newspaper is an exciting event. Mother had clipped out a recipe for lamingtons, my favorite sweet treat, and I had been allowed to keep the entire page of the comics and crossword puzzles. I was saving it for Sunday when I didn't have chores.

"Surely not," said Mother. "Not after the Great War. It was *the war to end all wars*. That's what was said over and over again when it ended." She poked her darning needle forcefully into the innocent sock. "The world is gone mad if it would allow such destruction and slaughter again."

Father did not reply but his grave expression did not lift.

Mother glanced at him now and again, a crease in her brow.

"If you are going to help me, Eleanor Margaret Dover," said Mother, "you best keep your eyes on what you are doing. No pinpricks and blood spots this time, young miss."

I had been looking out of the window, into the night, for I'd heard a noise.

"But did you hear that, Mother?" I asked. "Something is crying out there."

"Probably just the devils," said Mother, keeping her eyes on her darning needle. "They raise quite a ruckus when they squabble."

"It's not devils," I replied. "I know devil noise. It was different. It was like crying, or howling...so full of...of... sadness. Listen."

Both Father and Mother looked to the window for a few moments but nothing was to be heard above the cacophony of the crickets and cicadas.

"Back to your chores, miss, it's getting late now," said Mother. "Your imagination needs a rest."

"It wasn't my imagination, I heard it." I strained to hear the noise again. "It was so mournful. It almost had the quality of a musical note." I glanced to the window. "Can I go out and have a look?"

"Don't be daft, of course not," said Mother.

"Definitely not. What if it's a grizzly bear or a lion?" teased Father.

I giggled, happy to see Father broken from his somber mood.

"You know very well we don't have grizzly bears or lions in Australia, Father."

"No," he replied, turning back to his newspaper. "But we have hyenas that eat the sheep."

"Tasmanian tigers, you mean?" I asked him. "They aren't hyenas at all, Father, they are called thylacines, and they are marsupials. We learned about them in school. I saw one at the Hobart Zoo with Grandmother. His name was Benjamin."

"Oh, Eleanor! Heavens, look at what you've done!"

I looked to my lap. The white sock I was darning had a drip of red blood on it that was getting larger by the second. The blood was coming from my own finger. I'd pricked it with the darning needle and hadn't felt a thing.

13 January 1939

Oh joy! If I haven't gone and found a way to play! This afternoon, once I had peeled a mountain of potatoes, scrubbed the long table ready for supper, and chopped up enough carrots to sink a ship, mother said it would be fine for me to take a walk. The fresh air would do me good, she said, go and get some rose in my cheeks.

So I took the bush trail that Old Stevie the hunter uses, thinking I might catch sight of a wombat or a pademelon.

Maybe even discover the owner of the mysterious crying noise. I couldn't help but sing a tune as I walked. "Waltzing Matilda" always cheers my spirits.

The tips of the blue gums and lemon myrtle swayed above me as high as church steeples as I sang and strolled along, the sun trickling down through the branches, lighting my way.

A flash of red caught my eye and I bent down to peer beneath a mossy log and discovered a tiny ruby-red mushroom. The sweetest fairy toadstool as ever I saw! If I wait, I thought, perhaps I will see a fairy come to sit on her velvet throne.

So I continued to hum and tap my fingers on the old hollow log as I waited for the fairy before realizing the log itself carried a tune! It echoed and thumped under my fingertips. Not the real thing of course, but oh the joy to feel my fingers dance again. I played "Waltzing Matilda" on my hollow mossy log until the forest dimmed and the toadstool lost its brightness. I forgot all about keeping watch for the fairy.

The men were already sitting for supper when I rushed inside the dining hall. Mother gave me an awful scowl. I ignored her sour look and kissed her on the cheek because I had found such happiness!

19 January 1939

You will never ever guess what Old Stevie came back with today.

He returned from his hunting rounds while the piners were still out logging. He'd brought back two wood ducks and a fat possum for Mother and me to prepare for the men's dinner.

He also carried something else—something that wasn't dead because I could see it moving about in the sack.

"What is it, Stevie?" I asked him, pointing to his sack on the floor in front of the woodstove.

"I got meself a wee hyena pup," he said, lifting the little mite out of the sack. He dangled it in front of my face. "I reckon I'll take it to town and see what I can fetch for it. I heard a live pup can be sold for a good penny to zoos and such." He gave the pup a shake. "They say over in the Zeehan pub that the London Zoo paid £150 for a live adult tiger a ways back. It seems too daft to be true."

I took the poor weak creature from his rough grip. Its fur was smooth and its needle claws scratched at my arms as I held him against my chest.

"Oh, Stevie, however did you get him? He's a baby. Where is his mother?"

Old Stevie stood and shook his head. "He's not a joey anymore for he has his fur and he had already left the pouch. The mother got herself caught in my wallaby trap. Looked like she'd been there a good long while judging by the state of her. I shot her to end the misery. No use skinning her seeing as the government aren't paying the bounty anymore. But, like I said, I heard a live pup might fetch something." He tried to give the joey a scratch on its head but it opened its jaws wide in a show of fierceness.

My heart sank remembering the crying noise I'd heard a few nights before. It must have been the mother, caught in the trap. Or perhaps the baby, crying for his mother.

"Oh, the poor, poor creatures," I said.

Old Stevie just shrugged.

"And how awful to see this baby sold to a zoo like poor old Benjamin at Hobart. The correct name isn't a hyena, or tiger either, for that matter. It's a thylacine, Stevie, a marsupial, and it was a terrible thing for the government to put that bounty on their head and kill off so many. They are protected now. When Grandmother took me to visit Benjamin the Tasmanian tiger in the Hobart Zoo, I thought he was the saddest creature I had ever seen. And he died in that cage! Let this little lad at least live in freedom."

"Ah, he'd never survive on his own, lass. To be honest, I doubt he'll last out the night. At this age the mother still hunts for the young. It's likely he hasn't eaten for a long spell."

I pushed Old Stevie from the kitchen telling him that I would take care of the joey and keep him alive and that was that.

31 January 1939

I named the joey Shadow for his stripes remind me of the shadows cast by the giant tree ferns. Shadow loves possum heart and liver the best. He turns his nose up at anything else I try to feed him, especially if it is cooked, like lamb stew. It's only raw meat he likes and the bloodier the better. My little wildling! It makes sense, I suppose, because that would be what his mother would have provided. I don't believe for a second the tigers killed all the sheep they were accused of. It was surely the feral dogs instead, because it's wallaby and possum meat Shadow loves far more than any mutton or lamb I try to feed him.

He's growing to be a strapping little chap with his biscuit coat, chocolate stripes, and his odd stiff tail. I can understand why the thylacine has long been called a Tasmanian tiger, or a hyena, for the stripes are much the same. Shadow follows me around like a regular pup although his stride is quite clumsy. I suppose I am his mother now. I wonder if he misses his real mother and remembers her awful death? It doesn't bear thinking about. He is safe with me.

For the time being anyway.

Father says that, when all is said and done, the catch is Old Stevie's to do with as he wishes. If Old Stevie wants to sell Shadow to a zoo, or for his pelt, it is his property to do so with, and I mustn't make trouble when the time comes to give him back. Old Stevie agreed that I can raise Shadow until he is grown and then I must give him up. It is for Stevie to decide on what he will do with Shadow.

I try not to think about it.

Mother let me make a den for Shadow in the store shed and father said it was all right as long as I keep him out of the way of the piners. I put an old blanket down on the floor and he scratches at it for a long spell but usually settles eventually. He's restless at night because tigers are nocturnal. I am sure to lock the store shed so he doesn't go wandering in the dark. Nevertheless, he is eager to see me each morning and rubs his rough head against my legs and clambers over me with his sharp little claws.

Old Stevie made a kind of leash from old rope for me to use when I take Shadow on my bushwalks. Shadow sits like an angel when I hum and play my music. I daresay he likes the vibration of the hollow log. It makes him very calm and he always settles down when I sing and thump out the keys. He sits back on his hind legs, leaning on his stiff tail much like a kangaroo or a wallaby, and listens intently, blinking his large dark eyes as if to say, *I like your music.*

I am worried about leaving Shadow when we go home to Burnie for Easter. Old Stevie will stay at the camp and I can't trust that he won't try to sell Shadow like he said he would in the first place.

If only there were a safe place for Shadow, and other tigers, just like Professor Flynn proposed and as was reported upon in the newspapers a few years ago. He suggested then that a home should be provided for the endangered species on Maria Island. A sanctuary for the tigers, somewhere they would be out of harm's way, away from hunters and other dangers.

Sadly, the opposite has been the case with the bounty killing of most of the wild tigers and the rest left to wither in zoos. My mind turns over and over on how I can protect Shadow from either fate.

10 March 1939

I haven't written for weeks as I have been so busy with the chores and Shadow.

It gave me a mighty shock today, although I suppose it ought not to have, when Shadow trotted toward me with a possum in his mouth, just killed.

We had gone out on our regular bushwalk and I was humming my music as always. Usually Shadow sits and listens to the music, or curls up at my feet to sleep, but I suppose the dusk beckoned his wild nature. He scampered off, loose of his rope. He was gone only a short while before he came back and laid the dead thing at my feet. He sat for a moment before nudging the carcass toward me with his long snout. He sniffed and lapped at the blood. He seemed to offer it up as a gift. I took a step back and nodded. "You eat," I told him. "Go on." I could barely watch but could hardly drag my eyes away either. He sliced open the animal with surprising precision. Such sharp teeth! He proceeded to devour the choice bloody innards.

I sat some distance away, watching in fascination, pride, and ultimately great sadness. For I understood what it meant. It means he is grown and that I have fulfilled my promise and now must return him to Old Stevie.

The realization sends a shiver through me.

His fate is not mine to control. I cannot protect him any longer.

7

Eleanor's Journal
Part Two

"What happened to Shadow?" I demand of Uncle Ruff the next morning.

"Hm?" Uncle Ruff is listening to Piggy's heartbeat. She lies passively belly-up in his lap as he holds a stethoscope to her chest. I notice her unusually toed feet at the end of her spindly legs.

"What happened to Shadow when Eleanor went back to Burnie?" I ask.

"Oh. Well, that's where it all started really," he says, distracted, eyes on Piggy.

I tap my foot and look at him expectantly.

"The bushfire here in the '90s," he explains. "It burned

down the original camp." He points in the direction of a stretch of dirt the size of a basketball court. "That was where the dining hall and kitchen were originally." He waves his hand around his head. "What you see here now, these buildings, is all that was saved—just a few of the piners' cabins. Everything else went up in flames. Including her journal. Well, most of it."

I look around the camp with new eyes. I try to imagine the piners lining up for their dinner in their socks. I suddenly wish I could have seen the original buildings, as they were when Eleanor stayed here.

Uncle Ruff looks up. "Would you like to read more, Lou?" he asks quietly.

I have given up trying to get him to call me Louisa. "Yes. Do you have more?"

"Just one more set of pages. There's not much left, but it's enough." He looks back down at Piggy who is now crouched in his lap the right way up but not moving. "I just wanted to make sure you were interested in reading more before I gave it to you."

Being so keen to know what happened to Shadow, I hadn't noticed the sadness in Uncle Ruff's voice. I step closer and stroke Piggy. Her fur is rougher than I imagined and I wonder if Shadow's was the same. Piggy is so fragile that I can feel her thin bones beneath the coat.

"Is she any better?" I ask.

"She'll give us as long as she can," he says, cradling her in his hands before getting up and walking out to put her gently back in her pen. "But not much longer."

I feel like I should comfort him, like I imagine my mom or

Sophie would, but I can't think of anything to say.

"I'll get the journal," he says once he's settled Piggy gently onto her bed of straw. He goes to his room and returns with another plastic folder, which he hands me.

"Thank you," is all I manage to say.

I take the journal to the river's edge. The water laps rhythmically against a cluster of large boulders I climb onto. The winter sun provides a welcome warmth in the cool air. The winter temperature here is much like the fall in Toronto, or what Sophie describes as sweater weather. I sit with my legs stretched out on the rock and carefully take the journal out of the folder. As with the first set, the pages are wafer thin. The date on the front is 1942. Again, the journal pages have been photocopied and enlarged so the writing is easier to read.

Eleanor is older now, I realize, and her handwriting style has changed. Gone are the large loopy letters of her earlier years; now she writes in a precise, neat script. I begin reading, hoping to find out what happened to Shadow.

The journal of Eleanor Dover of Burnie, Tasmania.

11 November 1942

In the end it was Old Stevie who came up with the idea of

Convict Rock. I suspect he ended up feeling responsible after watching how attached I had become to Shadow. And no doubt he felt sorry about killing the mother.

Old Stevie is a bush man, with no manners to speak of, but I believe he is a good soul, and he confessed to me that he didn't have the heart to sell Shadow off to an unknown fate.

Back in 1939, in the weeks leading up to going home to Burnie for the Easter break, once I understood that Old Stevie didn't mean Shadow any harm, I talked to him about Professor Flynn's idea of the Maria Island sanctuary. I asked if it would be possible to take Shadow there, so he could be safe from hunters and traps.

"Maria Island is southeast, clear across Tasmania, as far as you can get from here in the northwest," he had scoffed. "Besides it were never agreed, just talked about, that sanctuary on Maria Island. Not one tiger lives there. Think how lonely he'd be."

"You are right, I suppose. Shadow should stay here where he can find a mate," I said. "But who is to say he'll find a mate here? Do you ever see other tigers around? You haven't caught more in your traps, have you?"

Old Stevie shook his head. "Not seen 'em. But I know there's more around. You can tell by the kills. They leave the animal mostly intact. Just take out the innards."

"Yes!" I agreed. "That's what Shadow did to the possum."

"The devils finish off the rest of the kill, I reckon," Old Stevie said.

"But if we let him free," I said, wringing my hands, "how

60

can I be sure he won't get caught in a trap or shot?"

Old Stevie had chewed his tobacco and pondered the quandary. He spat a dark wad on the dirt behind him. "No hunter will go over to Convict Rock on account of it's bad luck," he said rather mysteriously.

"Bad luck?! They don't go because they're scared." I chuckled. "It's just a bunch of silly superstitions and hogwash. Nothing will hurt you over there. Don't believe those cockamamie old-timey stories, Stevie." I prattled on for some time before I noticed the pointed look Old Stevie was giving me. "Oh. Yes, I see! No hunters on Convict Rock. I see, indeed! Could it be that we have our very own sanctuary right in front of our eyes?"

I sat and pondered this for a good long while.

"But...but...will he survive over there?" I asked Old Stevie. "How will he hunt and find a mate?"

"Tigers can swim, lass," said Old Stevie. "Used to watch 'em cross the Arthur River when I were a lad." He paused, thinking. "I reckon your Shadow, he'll swim out to hunt but he'll have somewhere safe to retreat."

"Could it really work, Stevie?" I ask. "Could Shadow really be safe over there?"

"Only one way to find out, lass."

It was chilly the afternoon when we set off in Stevie's skiff to Convict Rock. The water was so cold and clear you could see down to the smooth gray pebbles on the riverbed.

Shadow trembled against my legs in the boat. Being close to Stevie made him nervous for no doubt Shadow remembered his first and tragic encounter with him.

It had been easy enough to coax Shadow into the skiff. I held his rope with one hand and dangled a thick slice of possum meat with the other. Once we were settled on board, I let him gobble up the meat, and only after he'd finished eating did he become aware of his location and proximity to Stevie. I felt a pang of guilt for tricking him, for he trusts me so.

I held Shadow tightly by the rope as Stevie oared us over the river toward Convict Rock. I whispered to Shadow it was for his own good, but the closer we got to the rock the heavier my heart became. I wasn't ready to say goodbye, I wasn't ready to let him go! What if he became lonely and scared? What if he starved?

Shadow seemed to sense my unease and began to pant and yip and tug on the rope. He was restless, sniffing at the air with his long snout and pawing the side of the boat with his claws.

"Perhaps it's best if I spend a little time with Shadow on Convict Rock to make sure he finds a suitable den," I suggested to Stevie. When Stevie did not reply I went on. "I have become his mother, you see, and he trusts me. I just want to make sure he is safe there."

Stevie continued to row the skiff in silence. He looked skyward. The light was dimming and dusk was settling in. The last of the afternoon sun splashed across Convict Rock, which we now approached, a mere fifty yards away. Stevie rested the oars, stretched his arms, and took a swig of the water we had brought along.

"Let's discuss a plan, shall we?" I asked hopefully. "I really think it will be best if I take him ashore. That way he will feel secure. Then, once he is at ease, we can go back to the camp."

Old Stevie leaned toward me—I thought to try to give Shadow a pat, but before I could stop him, he had untied Shadow's rope, grabbed him by the scruff of the neck, and thrown him overboard.

"NO!" I shouted.

I leaned over the edge of the skiff and tried to reach for Shadow in the water, but Stevie gripped my arm tightly and settled me back on my seat. "Ya don't want to capsize us now, lassie."

"But why?" I blubbered. "Why did you do that?"

I scanned the river frantically. I could see Shadow's pointed ears and narrow snout above the water, heading toward Convict Rock.

"You don't want to make him soft," said Stevie, who was unmoved by my tears. "He's a wild animal. And he's gotta learn swimming is how he'll come and go from the place."

"But what if he drowns!"

Stevie pointed to Shadow. "Ya see his tail? That stiff tail acts like a rudder and will keep him straight in the current. He knows what he's doing."

Indeed, I had to admit, Shadow did not seem at all distressed in the water. He swam strongly and steadily, not troubled by the river's current.

Stevie and I bobbed around on the water in the skiff for a while longer before he picked up the oars and began to row us home. I sniffed and sobbed, continuing to watch as Shadow eventually reached the stony perimeter of Convict Rock. He shook himself briefly, much like a dog, then bounded out of eyesight, behind the cliffs.

He never looked back.

8

Eleanor's Journal
Part Three

*The journal of Eleanor Dover
of Burnie, Tasmania.*

12 November 1942

And that's how the sanctuary began. It was Old Stevie's doing.
I am writing of it now, all these years later, because the war
took over everything else. I am only now getting back into my
old habit of journaling.

On 3 September 1939, shortly after we had left Shadow

on Convict Rock, we listened to Prime Minister Menzies make the fateful announcement, over the radio, that Australia was at war. That was three years ago now and the camp stands empty, save for Mother and me, and Old Stevie. All the men, including Father, enlisted shortly after the prime minister declared war. Father made us promise that we would spend wartime in the bush, away from the city and any possible danger. It seems implausible that the fighting would find its way down here, to Tasmania, but we agreed in order to ease his mind. Besides, the food rationing has become so desperate in Burnie that it has benefited us to live out here where we can grow our vegetables and where Old Stevie can provide a steady supply of rabbit and wild duck for stew.

Grandmother has become quite the leader of the women's war effort back in Burnie. She has given over her house to the Red Cross and used it as the excuse why she sent the piano here. She claims the piano was taking up precious space needed for storing crucial Red Cross supplies, but I know in my heart that she sent it for me so I would not go mad with the isolation.

Old Stevie has a nephew fighting in the war. He is wounded now and Stevie has asked if he can convalesce here at the camp. Mother has agreed, of course. He will not be the first soldier we've taken in. It is the least we can do, she says. I know she wishes she could be back in Burnie or Devonport, helping with the war effort, but she will not break her vow to Father that we stay in the bush for the duration of the war. It is the first thing he asks in all his letters. He says it keeps him going, thinking of the two of us safe amongst the gums, sassafras, and pine, far away from the bullets and horrors of war. It gives him solace to think of his girls living in the peace of the forest.

After we dropped Shadow at Convict Rock three years ago, I had an awful time of it back in Burnie wondering and worrying about him. For the entire Easter break I kept telling myself that the arrangement was the best for Shadow, but I couldn't ease my own selfish need to see him and assure myself that he was healthy and well. As soon as I returned to the camp after Easter, I asked Old Stevie to take me over to the island in his fishing skiff to look for Shadow. Stevie complained that it would be useless to search because tigers sleep in the daytime and to disturb a den of tigers is foolishness itself, but he gave in to my pestering after a few days and rowed me over.

My search turned up nothing but scrapes and bruises from scrambling over rocks and boulders. If Shadow had made a den in one of the caves, I was useless to find it. The caves were either higher than I could climb or were buried where I could not see them. He did not respond to my calls or to the bag of possum meat I carried.

Old Stevie would not set foot on land and was adamant that he would leave me on Convict Rock if I insisted on staying after dusk. He denies it, of course, but I suspect that he believes in the old superstitions.

I spent a few mournful months searching the bush paths around the camp and making countless fruitless expeditions to

Convict Rock before I was to see Shadow again.

It was the music that lured him to me, I'm sure of it. By this time Grandmother had sent the piano and we placed it in the dining hall between two large windows overlooking the bush. I was playing "Waltzing Matilda" one evening after dinner, as was my habit.

As I played, I glanced out through the open window to the trees beyond. Suddenly I caught sight of movement under the giant tree ferns. I strained to see a shape in the dim light. Sure enough, there was my Shadow. He was sitting under the fronds listening to the music. He must have remembered the tune, for I used to hum it often when he was a pup.

I left the piano and walked down to his leafy hiding spot. He had become shy of me, as I now knew it should be. I crouched low and hummed the tune. After many moments he crept slowly toward me, his head low, sniffing my scent. He nosed my outstretched hand before opening his jaws wide to let me know he was now fully grown. He then sat back on his tail, blinking his large black eyes as if to say, *More music, please.* Or perhaps it was only the tasty morsel of rabbit meat that I had brought for him that held his attention. I'm not sure, and I didn't care. I was simply thrilled beyond measure to see him again.

Over the years that have followed, whenever I play the piano I know Shadow hears me, although he doesn't always come to visit.

So Old Stevie's idea of a sort-of tiger sanctuary at Convict Rock proved successful beyond my imaginings. Certainly, the war has helped. Although to attribute anything positive to the war feels wrong and disloyal to Father and all the men who are fighting as I write this. But the war certainly emptied the bush of its hunters.

I spend my time studying the forest and its animals. I walk the bush and take my field notes. Grandmother is a marvel at discovering a great variety of books and papers from public and private libraries. I pore over Darwin's volumes and Professor Flynn's papers. I daresay I have essentially put myself through a rigorous naturalist's degree. My favorite study subject of course is Shadow, and the other native animals.

A most joyous time came scarcely a year ago. One warm night Shadow sat under his ferns listening to the piano—but he was not alone! A smaller tiger sat with him. The females are smaller than the males. Shadow had found a mate and brought her to listen to the music.

Then, not six months ago, Old Stevie said he saw Shadow, his mate, and two pups taking a drink by the river's edge at dusk.

Indeed, this might have been the happiest moment of my life: to know that Shadow's tiger family was thriving in the wild. I swore again then, as I had done as a young lass, that I would do everything I could to keep them safe from harm.

But the truth is, I know this will be impossible.

The more I study, the more I understand that the native marsupials' habitat is in the greatest of peril. And none more so than that of our shy and majestic Tasmanian tiger.

I put down the pages and look across the river to Convict Rock. I ponder exactly what the pages are telling me. That the *extinct* Tasmanian tiger, Eleanor's tigers, might still exist on Convict Rock? But that's impossible. Eleanor said so much herself.

I'm keenly aware that I haven't picked up my violin for twenty-four hours, but I go back to Uncle Ruff's cabin. I want to know what happened after Eleanor's last journal entry—and what it means for the camp today. But I don't get a chance to ask because as I approach Uncle Ruff's cabin, I see his large frame hunched over Piggy's pen in the screened-in porch. He is silent but his shoulders shake in unmistakable grief.

Before I reach him, I know that Piggy is dead.

9

Old Battles

I'm not sure if Mel knows what has happened or whether it's just good timing on her part, but she's coming up the gravel drive in her SUV before I reach Uncle Ruff's cabin. He stands as he hears me open the screen door. He's cradling Piggy's lifeless body in his hands. Tears spill along his cheeks, run down his beard, and drip onto his shirt.

"Oh. I—I—" I stammer. "Is she—?"

He doesn't speak. He carries Piggy with him to the other corner of the porch and sits in his old armchair.

"Um. Can I do something?" I venture.

Uncle Ruff shakes his head.

"Go and help Colin," he manages to say after a few moments. "And tell Mel to come in here, please."

I do as I'm told, grateful to leave the uncomfortably sad scene. It's hard to watch my imposing uncle looking so completely undone. Before I open my mouth, Mel takes one look at my face, nods, and continues to walk past me toward Uncle Ruff's cabin.

"Take your stuff to Old Stevie's cabin," she says over her shoulder to Colin. "I'll come back and help in a minute."

Old Stevie's cabin! I turn my attention to Colin as he unloads his bags from the trunk. I had been so absorbed in my practicing, and in Eleanor's journal, that I'd almost forgotten about Colin. I feel apprehensive, not sure what to say or do.

"Are you going to help?" he asks.

I try to lift a suitcase from the trunk but it's too heavy for me to carry.

"What do you have in here?" I ask. "It weighs a ton."

Colin looks to see what I'm struggling with. "That suitcase contains my cookbooks and kitchenware. Its weight is possibly too heavy for you. I'll get Ruff to help me bring it in." He looks at the bag. "But it doesn't weigh anywhere near a ton," he says. "To be accurate, more like fifteen kilos."

"Piggy is dead." As I say the words, I know I sound cold-hearted. I wish I knew how to be nicer when emotional stuff happens.

"Oh. That's sad for Ruff," says Colin. "He must be very upset." But Colin's voice is almost robotic and his expression is blank, so it's hard to know if Colin really feels sad for Uncle Ruff or not.

He looks toward Uncle Ruff's cabin. Then he opens Old Stevie's cabin and peers inside. "Needs a good tidy-up," he says. He dumps his bags and turns to me. "Mum told me that you were a bit lonely here and that I should come over and stay." His large owl eyes meet mine for a second before he looks away. "Plus, you need someone to inform you about the Tarkine forest and Australia in general."

"Is that what she told you?" I ask.

He starts to tap his temple, ignoring my question. "I'd like to go and see how Ruff is doing."

We get to Uncle Ruff's porch and he's still sitting on his armchair holding Piggy. Mel is crouched in front of him with one hand on Piggy and one hand on his shoulder.

"Have you decided what you'll do with her?" she asks him.

"You know I have," he says. "It's never been in question. I'll bury her here on the property with the others. She'll return to the earth, to the land, just as she would have done a long time ago."

Mel stands up and sighs. "You need to do what you think is right, but I also feel like it's my responsibility to counsel you... to take time to consider what you're doing before it's too late."

"What do you think I've been doing these past months?" he says quietly.

"Yes. I know," says Mel kindly. "I just had to say it, that's all."

They both finally notice me and Colin standing at the screen door.

"Time to say goodbye to Piggy," Mel says, holding out her arms to us.

Uncle Ruff spends the rest of the day digging a very deep hole on the slope behind the cabins.

"It's so no scavengers will eat her," Colin says matter-of-factly when I ask why the grave has to be so deep.

"Gross," I say.

Colin blinks at me without expression. "I don't believe scavenging can be described as gross. To be accurate, it is an essential part of the ecosystem. Animals like Tasmanian devils act as efficient garbage collectors, consuming dead carcasses of all kinds, including the bones, fur, and cartilage."

"Okay, we get the picture. Thanks, love," says Mel.

Ruff waves off any offers of help. He obviously wants to do the task alone.

Mel and I manage to get the suitcase of cookware hauled to the kitchen and we unpack it while Colin cleans out his cabin.

I look for drawer space to put Colin's many knives, wooden spoons, and various other utensils in an assortment of shapes and sizes. "Does Colin really need all this stuff?" I ask.

Mel chuckles. "Apparently he does," she says. "Don't worry, you'll be grateful once you get used to his cooking." She pauses. "A few things it will be helpful to know," she says. "Routine is very important to Colin. He'll keep to his own schedule, but he knows not to expect others to keep the same routine." Mel continues her unpacking. "And just because you might not see him express it, doesn't mean he is not feeling emotions. Sometimes he feels intensely and he needs to be alone to calm down from the emotional overload." She looks up and smiles. "So if he spends a lot of time in his cabin, don't worry."

"I won't worry," I say.

"Sorry. I'm probably blabbing on too much about him. It's a habit."

"It's okay," I say. Then I change topics. "Can I ask you something? You called Colin's cabin Old Stevie's cabin?"

"Yep. Old Stevie lived here a long time ago. He was your great-great-uncle or something like that."

"No. Eleanor was my great-grandmother. Old Stevie was just the hunter and caretaker."

"So you don't know about Freddie yet?" Mel asks.

"No, who's Freddie?"

"Freddie was your great-grandfather," she replies. "Eleanor's husband. Freddie was Old Stevie's nephew."

I remember reading in Eleanor's journal about Old Stevie's nephew coming to stay at the camp. "Wow. So Freddie is the nephew who was injured in the war?" I ask. "I'm actually related to Old Stevie?"

"That's right. Freddie came here to convalesce in 1942 and never left. Eleanor and Freddie fell in love and stayed here their whole lives. Sadly, poor Freddie didn't live to be an old man. But he was the one who gave Eleanor her first pair of pig-footed bandicoots. Old Stevie had told him about Eleanor's interest in endangered animals. He was billeted to a hospital in Western Australia after he was injured. Somehow during his time there he had happened upon a pair of bandis that were injured.

Freddie thought the camp would be a good place for them. And he was right."

"There's a lot to know about this place," I say.

Mel adds a thick cookbook to a stack on the bench beside the kitchen table. "There is," she agrees. "But it's best if I let your uncle tell you most of it."

"Can you just tell me one thing," I say. "What did you mean earlier when you asked Uncle Ruff if he was sure he was doing the right thing?"

Mel sits on a kitchen chair. "Are you sure your mum didn't tell you about any of this?" she asks.

"I think she tried," I admit.

"Well, okay," she says. "I was asking him if he wanted to give Piggy's body to the scientific community. Pig-footed bandicoots are thought to have been extinct since the 1950s. There are many experts in the field who would be ecstatic to study her."

"So why is he burying her here? Shouldn't he preserve her or something until they can study her?"

"No, that's the point. He will not share Piggy, or anything about Eleanor's legacy, with anyone."

"But why?" I ask. "It doesn't make sense."

"That's how your mum felt too. She strongly believed that the observations made here at the camp should be shared with the scientific community. Rufus disagreed, and still does."

"Wait," I say. "Is that why my mom left Tasmania?"

"That's really something only your mum can answer, but I can tell you that when the decision was left to your mum and

76

Rufus about what to do with the camp, Rufus wanted to keep it going in the same tradition that Eleanor had started. For the animals to be left alone."

Mel pauses and glances out the window. "So your mum finished her degree and went to Canada. She met your dad soon after, had you girls, and built a career she loves. So you could definitely say the story has a happy ending."

"But not for Uncle Rufus," I say. "The camp is being torn down for the mining road."

Mel nods sadly. "It's true. There isn't anything we can do about losing the camp. That battle was fought long ago, and we lost." She sighs. "But Rufus has managed to keep Eleanor's tigers safe here—" Mel stops abruptly as if she has said more than she intended.

"I've read Eleanor's journals. Are you trying to say there are still tigers on Convict Rock?" I ask.

Mel looks out the window again, to where Ruff is digging. "Come on. I think Ruff has finished Piggy's grave," she says.

Mel turns to me, her voice low. "It's better if your uncle tells you about the tigers."

10

Goodbye, Piggy

I thought we would have some kind of ceremony to bury Piggy, but Uncle Ruff shakes his head when Mel offers to say a few words. We are all standing around the deep, deep hole that Uncle Ruff has dug. He is holding Piggy, now wrapped in a cotton pillowcase that Mel found. He has sweat pouring down his face. He looks worn out.

He takes off his hat and crouches to lower Piggy into the grave. "Goodbye, girl," he says quietly, holding his hat to his chest.

"Come on, kids," says Mel. "Let's give Ruff some time alone to say goodbye."

"Goodbye, Piggy," says Colin, letting Mel lead him away.

Once we're inside Uncle Ruff's cabin, Colin busies himself in the kitchen, rearranging the cookware that Mel and I had put away.

"Don't be surprised if Ruff goes to the pub and stays the night," says Mel. "They'll make sure he doesn't drive if he has too many beers."

"Okay, thanks," I say. "We'll be all right."

"Of course you will, I don't doubt it for a second," she says, glancing at Colin. "I have to get back to the Eco Lodge now. Colin knows how to reach me on the shortwave radio if anything comes up." She stands to leave. "Take care of each other," Mel tells us.

"Bye, Mum," Colin says. His arm waves above the counter, his head still buried in a cupboard.

"Thank you," Mel whispers to me, and I nod. Mel has a way of making me feel more grown-up than I am.

I watch through the window as Mel and Uncle Ruff talk. Standing by her SUV, before she drives away. I want to talk with Uncle Ruff too. I want to ask him about Convict Rock and the tigers, but I can see it is not a good time to get his attention.

Instead I go to my cabin and practice. I'm lost in my mistakes until something, maybe the vibration of the music, triggers tears. I cry silently, unable to erase the image of Uncle Ruff cradling Piggy's frail, lifeless body in his arms.

I find an old piece of sheet music for a song I don't play anymore and that's blank on one side. I fold it into a card. On it I write:

Dear Uncle Ruff,
I'm sorry for your loss.
Piggy was very sweet.
Love, Louisa.

Sophie helped me write a card like this when Alicia's beloved dog died. I take the card to Uncle Ruff's cabin to leave somewhere he'll find it.

As soon as I step into the porch the aroma of Colin's cooking wafts through the screen door.

"Whatever you're cooking smells amazing," I say as I enter the cabin. It's warm and cozy, with a fire blazing. I stand in front of the grate and warm my hands against the glowing flames.

"It's just shepherd's pie," says Colin. He's sitting on a kitchen stool, with one of his cookbooks open on the counter in front of him. "There's plenty left if you are hungry. I already ate with Ruff before he went to the pub. We didn't want to interrupt your music."

"Thanks," I say. "It's just practice. I hope it didn't sound too awful."

"I liked it. I enjoyed listening," he says earnestly.

"I'm having trouble getting back in rhythm since I got here."

Colin shrugs and returns to reading his book.

I slip into Uncle Ruff's bedroom and prop the condolence card on his pillow before going to the kitchen and spooning a generous serving of Colin's shepherd's pie onto a clean plate.

"Tomato sauce is in the fridge," he says.

"Tomato sauce?" I ask.

"You probably call it ketchup."

"Oh, right," I say. "Thanks."

I go to the fridge and squeeze a dollop of ketchup onto the plate before sitting at the kitchen table. "This is good," I say between mouthfuls of creamy potato and tender beef filling.

"It's nothing special," he replies. "To be accurate, shepherd's pie is often described as peasant food."

We look at each other and I chuckle.

"I guess we have something in common," I say. "Neither of us is very good at taking compliments."

"My mum would call it an icebreaker," says Colin, closing his cookbook.

"So you like to cook, huh?" I ask.

"Yes, it's one of my special interest subjects. It is very precise. If I follow the recipes there is a predictable outcome. It's not complicated." He fixes me with his owl-like eyes for a moment before looking away. "And you like to play the violin."

"I want to be a violinist. I'm practicing for a big audition to get into the youth symphony orchestra back in Toronto when I get home. I want it more than anything."

"Will you get it?" he asks.

"I don't know. I need to practice. I need to be perfect this time." I stop and look out the window. "In the past, I—I haven't done so well with auditions."

Colin doesn't reply, but I like that he doesn't try to tell me it will be fine.

He taps at his temple. "I know why Mum wants me to stay

here," he says. "I'm not stupid. I wanted to go along with it to make her happy."

I keep eating, not knowing what to say.

"Just as long as you know you don't have to pretend to like me," he says.

"I wouldn't—I mean, I won't." Colin's honesty is disarming. My face flushes as I remember my reaction when Mel first asked if he could come and stay.

"I get it," says Colin. "I'm creepy. I'm a weirdo."

"Don't say that."

"It's what I hear people our age say. Plus, it's accurate that I'm not like most of the other kids at school. I talk too much, too loudly, or I don't talk at all. I spend time alone reading or cooking when other kids are playing sports or hanging out together. I don't have any friends. Not since Mick."

"Maybe we're not so different," I say. "I babble when I'm nervous. And we both prefer solo activities."

Colin looks like a light has been lit inside him. His hand drops to his side. "I knew there was a reason why it is easy to talk to you," he says. "You understand."

"So tell me about Mick," I ask, and his glow disappears. I wish I could take it back. "Sorry. You don't have to tell me."

Colin begins to tap again. "I used to have a friend called Mick. We were friends since kindergarten. We did many activities together, bushwalks, fishing, sleepovers. Then, during the holidays between year six and year seven, he started spending time with the townie kids, playing football and going to parties." He pauses. "Over an approximate six-day period he stopped being my friend."

"He sounds like a jerk," I say.

"No. He isn't a jerk at all. He is nice. Mum says I can't blame him for wanting to have other friends and do other activities." He folds his hands together; I imagine in an effort to stop himself from tapping and fidgeting. "I don't like to go to parties or play football, so it puts me at a disadvantage to continuing the friendship."

"Is there anyone else at school you like? That you want to be friends with?"

He glances at me briefly. "Since starting high school—in Australia we start high school in year seven—it has been difficult for me to make friends because there are a lot of people I don't know...I'm not sure who I can trust."

"Just feed them your shepherd's pie," I say, holding a forkful in the air. "Everyone will love you."

"Thank you," he says. "It's a strategy I could possibly adopt. I will think about it."

"Can I ask you something?"

"Yes."

"Do you know anything about the Tasmanian tigers that used to live here? I've been reading my great-grandmother's journal. She raised a tiger joey called Shadow here back in the 1940s and apparently they used Convict Rock as a kind of sanctuary. Do you know what happened to them?"

"I thought you knew," he said.

"Knew what?"

"About this camp," he says. "About keeping Tasmanian tigers at Convict Rock. It's what your family have always done."

"Wait. You mean, like *still*? Like...*now*?"

Colin nods and my heart races.

"Have you ever—ever actually *seen* one?" I stammer.

"Would you like to see the cell phone video I got of one?"

I nod, barely able to believe what he's saying.

Colin takes his cell phone from his pocket and taps at the screen. "Here," he says, passing the phone to me. "Look."

I watch the small screen. The video is grainy but I can make out the shape of a ground fern along a bush trail. The video moves abruptly from left to right. I hear excited whispering from the recording. "*There! Look!*" The focus zooms in beneath the fern. From the shadowy space two large eyes meet the camera. In a flash the eyes are gone; the animal turns and runs away. Colin takes the phone back and pauses the frame. He enlarges the shot and passes the phone back to me. "See," he says, pointing. "You can see the tiger stripes."

The still frame clearly captures distinct dark stripes along the back of the animal, but I'm still not sure what I'm looking at.

"That was taken one year and nine months ago," says Colin. "Mum and I were hiking nearby. We were hoping to observe a quoll that had been spotted near there, but we saw a Tasmanian tiger instead."

"Didn't you ever want to show it to someone? I mean, like, the authorities?" I ask.

"There is no point. This video is not proof. The quality is not good and the image is not clear. Rangers would likely say it was a wild dog." He puts his phone away. "But Mum and I know what we saw."

"I can't really tell what I'm seeing," I say. "I mean, I don't really know what they look like."

Colin takes his phone back out and taps the screen again. He holds the screen so I can see. It's another video and this time I can tell from the black-and-white image that it's an old recording. I watch as a striped creature paces back and forth on the screen. It looks like a wild dog, but then again it looks like nothing I've ever seen. It gives the impression of being both powerful and fragile at the same time. It opens its jaws wide, showing impressive rows of teeth. Its huge dark eyes settle on the camera, an expression so searching and forlorn that it squeezes my heart.

"That's a historic film of Benjamin," says Colin. "He was the last-known Tasmanian tiger held in captivity. He died of exposure in the Hobart Zoo on September 7, 1936."

I can't take my eyes from the screen. It's as if Benjamin—or Shadow—is reaching out to me from back in time. A time now lost. I stare at this mysterious animal and feel his plight, his anguish, just as my great-grandmother had written about in her journal all those years ago.

"Hello again," I whisper.

11

Lost

In the bush, night falls quickly. As I step down from Uncle Ruff's porch to go back to my cabin, I'm struck by the sudden darkness, and in contrast, the breathtakingly beautiful star-lit sky.

I breathe in the cool night air as I wander down the dirt driveway to find a clearing so I can take a better look at the nightscape. I remember Sophie telling me that when she was here she would find the Southern Cross constellation every night. I keep my eyes above, searching for something that looks like a cross. The sky is freckled with millions and millions of stars, pulsating flecks and pinpoints of twinkling light. It is mesmerizing. I keep walking with my eyes on the stars, searching for a pattern in the constellations, for the famous Southern Cross that is featured on the Australian flag.

A whack of fern fronds hits me in the face. I push them away and find my hands grabbing at the rough spines of a giant tree fern. I spin around. Somehow, I've wandered off the driveway and into the forest. *Don't panic*, I tell myself. *You can't have gone far.* I look around me, but I can't see a thing. My eyes have been focused on the light of the stars, now they aren't working in the darkness around me. I can't even see my hands. "Don't panic." I say it aloud this time. But I can't help it—I do panic. I push branches aside and rush in one direction and then the next, but I can't find my way out. It feels as if the branches, leaves, and fronds are trying to tangle me up and trap me. I keep stumbling and pushing through the foliage. I start remembering all the snakes, spiders, and fungi I read about. All the poisonous and deadly creatures that live in this forest and that can bite, sting, and kill you. I run as fast as I can but suddenly smack into a thick tree trunk. The blow acts like a slap, breaking me from my hysteria. I slump to the base of the gum, leaning my back against the knobby bark. I rub my forehead.

What am I doing here? How am I going to get back? What if I can't get out? What if I'm trapped here? My mind races. Then I hear panting. Short bursts of heavy panting, just like a dog. *Your mind is playing tricks*, I tell myself. *It's just your own breath.*

But I keep hearing it, rhythmic panting, not too far away, but not too close either. I think of Shadow and the video Colin showed me of Benjamin.

I feel the presence of something watching me. I am sitting in the pitch-dark and something is there, watching me.

"HELP! COLIN! HELP ME! I'M LOST! PLEASE HELP ME!" I scream over and over until my throat is dry and hoarse.

The night is silent now and I feel alone. Whatever was or wasn't there has been scared off by my screaming.

Eventually I hear a new noise, the cracking and snapping sound of twigs stepped on by firm human footsteps, and I see the glorious sight of a flashlight beam.

"I'm here! Here!" I shout, standing up and jumping up and down. "Colin, I'm here!"

Colin reaches me and casts the flashlight up and down my body. "I heard you yelling," he says.

"That was the idea," I say.

"Are you hurt?" he asks.

"No. I don't think so," I say. "Just a little freaked out."

"What are you doing out here?" he asks.

"I'll explain later, please just lead me back to the camp."

"Put your hand on my shoulder," says Colin calmly. He leads me the short distance back to the driveway. I can't believe how close I was to the camp the whole time.

"It is definitely not recommended for hikers to walk in the bush at night," Colin offers. "Especially for someone as inexperienced as you are. There is the issue of poor visibility, of course, and therefore a significant spike in the possibility of becoming lost, injured, even drowning. If a disoriented hiker stumbles and falls into a dam or swift-moving river—"

"Okay, okay, I get it, thanks," I say, interrupting him. "I didn't *want* to go for a hike, I just wanted to find the Southern Cross. It's stupid, I know. I was looking up at the sky and the next thing I know, I was surrounded by bush." I'm embarrassed to tell him about the panting noise and that I thought a creature was watching me.

"The Southern Cross constellation, you mean?" he asks.

I nod, and Colin turns to face the opposite direction, back toward Uncle Ruff's cabin, back the way I had come.

"The Southern Cross constellation is found on the southern horizon. You were looking in the wrong direction. You were heading toward the north."

"Figures," I say.

Colin points to the sky. "The Southern Cross is located near the larger constellation Centaurus. To find the Southern Cross, first you find two very bright stars, Alpha and Beta Centauri, they are the pointers. Following the line from Alpha and Beta Centauri will lead you to Gamma Crucis, the top star in the Southern Cross crux." He pauses. "Do you see it?" he asks, still pointing.

I nod, not sure at all that I'm looking at the right stars, but listening to Colin's steady monologue is incredibly comforting after feeling so wildly frightened just moments before. I listen to him talk while my heart gradually slows to normal.

"The Southern Cross is composed of four stars, Gacrux, Delta, Acrux, and Mimosa, forming the shape of a cross, or to be more accurate, the shape of a kite. A fifth star between Delta and Acrux is called Epsilon, but more recently known as Ginan, its Aboriginal name. Acrux and Gacrux point in the direction of the southern celestial pole."

"Oh, wait!" I say suddenly. "I see them!" I wave at the inky sky where I can now clearly see the four-pointed shape of a kite. "Right there!"

"Affirmative," says Colin, turning his flashlight off. "It is optimal to observe stars without any other light source. The stars that make up the Southern Cross," he continues, "are estimated to be between ten and twenty million years old. In the southern hemisphere the Southern Cross is frequently used for navigation, much like the star Polaris, also called the North Star, is used in the northern hemisphere, where you are from."

We keep watching the stars and I marvel at how far from home I really am. Even the night sky is foreign. I am totally upside down. No wonder I got lost.

"Thank you," I say. "Thank you for finding me, and thank you for showing me the Southern Cross."

"You are welcome," he replies. "And now that you know how to find it yourself, you won't get lost again."

"I hope not."

"I'll walk you to your cabin," he says. "Just in case."

Colin waits patiently outside the cabin while I light the kerosene lamp and give him the thumbs-up from the window so he'll know that I'm okay. He already checked for spiders with his flashlight. I slip under the covers and watch through the cabin window as the shaft of light from Colin's flashlight bobs and weaves its way to his cabin; the same cabin that was once Old Stevie's.

I lie under the covers, relieved to be safe again, picturing the Southern Cross constellation blinking high above me. But I can't shake the feeling I had in the bush.

That something was out there in the dark, watching me.

12

The First Bandicoots

When I wake up the next morning, Uncle Ruff's jeep is still not back. I put in my earbuds and listen to one of Bach's sonatas for violin on my iPod before walking over to Uncle Ruff's cabin. The air smells like fresh bread.

I take out my earbuds. "Did you bake?" I ask Colin, who is sitting on the porch steps, putting on his boots. "Something smells fantastic."

"I baked oats for muesli. It's inside if you want some." He throws a knapsack over his shoulder. "I'm going foraging." He looks at me. "Do you want to come?"

I shake my head. "Foraging for what?" I ask.

"Food. Foraging is the acquisition of food by hunting, fishing, or gathering plant matter. To be accurate, I'll be focusing exclusively on plant matter."

"No thanks, I'll stay here and wait for Uncle Ruff. I want to ask him about the tigers."

"Roger that."

Before going inside, I watch Colin as he walks away along the riverbank.

I've made tea and eaten two bowls of Colin's homemade muesli when Uncle Ruff's jeep pulls into the camp. I watch through the window as he walks from his jeep to Piggy's burial site. He stands with his head down and his hat held at his chest, swaying slightly. He stays like this for a while. As he starts to walk toward the cabin, I quickly move away from the window and pour a mug of tea.

"Smells like Colin has been busy," I hear him say as he enters the porch.

"Tea?" I ask.

"Don't mind if I do," he says. He plonks himself down on a chair at the kitchen table and I place the hot mug in front of him.

"How was the pub?" I ask. He looks like he slept in his clothes, but he seems surprisingly rested.

"Just what I needed," he says, taking a sip of his tea. "Never underestimate the great healing power of a few beers with mates at the pub. Australian therapy, we call it."

I'm pleased to see he's in lighter spirits.

"Mmm," he adds appreciatively. "That's good tea." He nods at me over the steam of his mug. "You have a lump on your forehead."

"Oh, this," I say, rubbing my bump. "It's nothing, just a run-in with a gum tree. I'm fine."

"Aha," he says with a wink and a smile. "That happens around here sometimes." He takes another sip of tea. "Are you sure you're okay?"

I nod yes.

"I'm guessing you finished reading Eleanor's journal?" he asks.

"Yes," I say, sitting across from him at the table. "And Colin showed me his video of a tiger sighting."

"Ah. Okay," he says, "so the cat's out of the bag...or the tiger, we should say." He chuckles at his own joke.

"Will you tell me about Convict Rock?" I ask. "Colin said our family have always hidden tigers. What happened after Eleanor's last journal entry?"

Uncle Ruff leans back in his chair. "Okay," he says, "let's start with Freddie. Your great-grandfather Freddie, Old Stevie's nephew. He arrived soon after that journal entry and he brought with him a pair of injured pig-footed bandicoots."

I settle in and listen.

"At the time, 1942, pig-footed bandis were endangered. They lived in semi-arid areas of the country but had experienced rapid decline early in the century. Most likely due to the introduction of cats, dogs, and foxes from the European settlers. As well as the animal's habitat being cleared for farming.

It's the same story for most of the endangered and extinct marsupials in this country—the introduction of invasive predators and the destruction of natural habitat—it equals disaster for the native species. By 1950 the piggies were declared extinct.

"Eleanor and Freddie wanted to establish an insurance population of the species, first in captivity, then with the goal of reestablishing a healthy population in the wild."

"So the pair of bandis Freddie brought here were Piggy's ancestors?" I ask.

"They were. Freddie and Eleanor nursed the sick pair back to health. Pretty soon they had a litter. At some point Eleanor and Freddie introduced the southern brown bandicoots to the piggies to establish the critical mass population needed to keep the hybrid species going. By that stage the bandis were living all around the camp."

"It sounds like it was a success," I say.

"It was," says Uncle Ruff. "For many, many years. Until the same problem found them. Feral dogs and the destruction of their habitat. By the early '90s, the population had become dangerously low. Eleanor caught a mating pair of piggies as insurance. It made her sad that she had to keep them in captivity again, but she was determined to try and save them as she had done way back during the war. But it didn't work as it had the first time. For any species to survive there needs to be critical mass to sustain the gene pool. The population slowly dwindled, until..."

"Until Piggy," I say. "She was the last one?"

"Yep. The southern brown bandis are still about. But no

more piggies. And soon, no more camp." He stops and looks out the window for a moment. "Time is up for the camp." He sighs. "The local government have approved the bridge across the Pieman River. It's what the miners want. They can move their tin and iron ore more efficiently if they can drive it over the river instead of driving around it. The bridge will travel straight across Convict Rock. They plan to dynamite it. It's the most direct line from here to reach the main roads. Since before the war there hasn't been access across the river."

"But why are they allowed to build a bridge here, on our land?" I ask.

"It's not our land, as it turns out. Well, there's no document to prove it anyway. Eleanor's father was the foreman and care-taker of the camp. It's unclear who actually owned the land, but it seems our family was only entrusted to take care of it. The pulp mill in Burnie claimed they owned it but couldn't provide land deeds. Long before that, it was a mining camp. With no evidence of legal ownership, land returns to the government."

"It's not fair," I say.

"Depends on how you look at it. The camp is here in the first place because of mining. In the mid-1800s, gold was found in the area and it sparked a mini–gold rush. The gold rush pe-tered out before long, but exploration of the area found tin and silver. So mining continued to boom until the early 1900s. When the mining slacked off, the logging took up. The federal government finally protected the forests from logging—well, some of them, for a time—but now the chainsaws are back." He takes a slurp of his now-cold tea. "Tasmania will always be divided by the townies and greenies. People who need to make a living, that's the townies—and greenies, people like Mel, who want to save the environment." He pauses. "Besides, if you really want to talk about 'fair,' long before mining or logging, the land rightfully belongs to the Aboriginal people. But it was taken from them."

I recall what I'd heard Mel telling the tourists at the Eco Lodge about the Aboriginal people being the rightful owners of all the land. Then I think back to my bus journey and to the vast tracts of cleared land I saw alongside the road. It was probably caused by logging or mining, I realize now.

"And the tigers?" I ask.

I hold my breath, waiting for his answer.

Uncle Ruff gets up from his chair. "Come with me," he says.

13

Tiger Whisperer

As I follow Uncle Ruff out of the cabin, Colin is walking up from the river. He cradles bunches of glossy, lime-colored leaves in his arms.

"What have you got there?" I ask.

"River mint," he answers, holding a bunch to my nose. It smells fresh and pepperminty. "I found some native pepper-berry as well," he goes on, pointing to his knapsack. "They are excellent to use fresh. Or you can dry the berries and grind them up."

Ruff lifts his chin. "Put that stuff inside, mate, and come with us," he says.

Colin drops his knapsack and the herbs on the cabin steps and rejoins us.

"Where are we going?" he asks. I shrug because I'm truly not sure where we're going either.

We follow Uncle Ruff along the riverbank in the opposite direction from where Colin went foraging. We skirt the rear of my cabin and continue along the river for twenty minutes or so until we reach a stretch of sandy shore. The bush behind the shore is dense. It appears the only way to reach this point on the river is from the camp. The shoreline is interrupted by an outcrop of large rocks jutting into the water. To continue walking would mean a vertical climb, twenty feet up and over the rock face, or wading into the deep river.

Uncle Ruff stops walking and looks out over the water toward Convict Rock. "This is where the tigers usually cross," he says matter-of-factly, and my heart starts to pound at what I'm hearing. "Used to anyway," he says. "Now I can't be 100 percent sure. For a long time, I've only seen single prints. Small, so likely a female. Then nothing at all for a while now. If she is still here, she is alone."

I am speechless.

"Mum told me," says Colin. "She said that you haven't had a sighting in a long time."

Uncle Ruff nods. "It has been a long time. Maybe over a year. My guess is that she was injured so the pack left her behind."

"There was a pack?" I ask.

"There was. About two years ago they took off, deeper into the bush. I was happy at the time because I knew about the proposed mining road and what will happen to Convict Rock.

It was like the pack knew too, although of course they couldn't have." He looks thoughtful. "Besides, it's happened many times before—the tigers from the Rock going deeper into the Tarkine for better hunting or to find mates. At some point a pair would come back to the Rock and the cycle would start over." He pauses. "But Ellie has no hope if she's alone."

"Ellie?" I ask.

"That's what I call her. Short for Eleanor. The one and only." He points behind us into the bush. "I built a trap months ago," he says. "But she's too smart for me."

I peer at where he's pointing. All I can see are the densely curled fronds of ground ferns, but on closer inspection I notice the outline of a wire cage.

"Why don't you just go to Convict Rock and look for her?" I ask.

"I've looked dozens of times. She's too elusive," says Uncle Ruff. "Or maybe it's true about the Rock," he says.

"What do you mean?"

"In all the years since Shadow was first taken to Convict Rock, no one has ever actually found a den or seen a tiger on the Rock. It's like the tigers become ghosts over there. That's what Old Stevie used to say—that the tigers survive there because the Rock is haunted and the ghosts protect them."

We look out over the river toward the rocky outline of the narrow island. Mist is hovering below the tops of the cliffs, giving it an eerie and mysterious appearance.

"Or, more likely, her den is underground and that's why I can't find it," says Uncle Ruff.

"But if you trap her, what will you do with her?" I ask.

"Take her to a more remote area of the forest where she has a hope of joining other tigers. If she stays here, once the road construction starts, she'll be killed—or seen and discovered, which in my opinion means the same thing. The entire world would descend upon the Tarkine looking for more like her."

"Do you know where you'll take her?" I ask.

"Mel will ask the Aboriginal elders. They have knowledge of the land and the environment in a way that we could never have. Their ancestors lived alongside the tigers for thousands of generations, they'll know where she will be safe. That's all we'll ever need to know. It's better that way."

Colin is busy investigating the trap. "The probable reason you haven't caught her," he says, "is because the wire at the back of the trap has a hole in it."

"It does?" says Ruff. "I haven't given it too much attention lately, I've been busy with Piggy."

"So other people know about the tigers here?" I ask them both. "I mean...you guys, and Mel, and the Aboriginal elders?"

"You'd be surprised how many people can keep a secret. Especially Tasmanians," says Ruff. "There are a few reasons," he goes on. "Some folks are of the same mind-set as me and Eleanor—that after the way the early settlers treated the tigers, they should be left alone. Others, who might catch a glimpse of a tiger, don't report it because to do so carries with it a certain amount of ridicule. It's like saying you've seen Bigfoot or the Loch Ness Monster—people think you're nuts. All the evidence points to the fact that they do not exist. And many, many sightings of tigers over the years have been proven false. So a lot of folks just keep quiet about it. It's our way."

"But I remember my dad writing about scientific expeditions that didn't show any evidence of tigers, how is that possible?" I ask.

"Probably the devils. Devils are hunters but mostly scavengers. They eat the entire carcass of an animal, hair, bones, and cartilage. The devils forage in the same habitat as the tigers, so it's likely they gobble up any clues of tiger remains. Besides, the Tarkine is so vast, there's no way it could be explored completely. You could probably hide a triceratops here if you really wanted to."

"But you don't know for sure if Ellie is still here?" I ask.

"I haven't seen tracks, scat, or any evidence for a while. I'd almost given up hope until you got here."

"Me?" I ask, surprised.

"Yep, you."

"But how?" I ask. "Why me?"

Uncle Ruff scratches his beard and we see the beginning of a smile. "It would appear that Ellie is a curious girl. She came exploring the camp the first night you arrived, to check out your scent."

"How could you know that if you haven't seen her or her tracks?" I ask.

"Because you told me," he said.

I flap my arms in exasperation. "I don't understand."

"The smell," he said finally. "You told me you woke up in the night and there was an awful smell." He taps his nose. "It could only have been Ellie."

"But couldn't it have been devils?" Colin asks. "They make a pungent smell when they're stressed."

Ruff shakes his head. "We have discouraged devils from making dens at the camp for decades because of the bandis. Besides, if the smell came from a devil, it could only mean the same thing. That a larger predator was there, and the only predator larger than the devil is the tiger."

He puts his hand on top of my head. "Nope. I'm certain of it. Lou here is our tiger whisperer."

14

A Trip to Town

While Colin is at work in the kitchen, washing the native berries and mint from his foraging mission, I ask Uncle Ruff to tell me more about Eleanor.

"What was she like?" I ask him. "I mean, like, as a person."

"Eleanor?" asks Uncle Ruff. "Oh, she was smart, strong, and funny. She worked hard and loved the land. And the animals, of course. She was passionate about the native animals. She never had a formal university education, but she knew more about the bush and the environment than anyone I know. During the day she would be out in the forest, making her observations, and every night she would play the piano." He pauses, thinking.

"She wasn't just one thing, she didn't fit into a box. You couldn't label her. She was unique and lived her life exactly how she wanted it."

"And Freddie?" I ask.

"Poor old Freddie died of tuberculosis after the end of the war. He barely lived long enough to meet their daughter, Kathleen," he says. "Our mother—your grandmother."

"Was your mom like Eleanor?"

"Not at all," says Ruff, with a shake of his head. "She was a city girl through and through, our mum. Eleanor always said Kathleen took after Eleanor's grandmother."

"It was Eleanor's grandmother who gave her the piano and sent her the books, right?" I ask.

"Yes, that's right. Eleanor played beautifully." He gives me a pointed look. "Just like someone else I know."

I blush.

He laughs. "You didn't think your talent came from nowhere, did ya, Lou?" he says.

"Well, I didn't think it came from the Tasmanian rain forest," I say.

"That's fair enough," he says. "But you are *fair dinkum* great at that violin of yours, Lou." He stops. "Do you know what fair dinkum means?"

"I think so," I say, but I'm not at all sure.

"Well, it means the *real deal*."

"Thanks," I say.

Later we decide to go into town for groceries after Colin complains of having no fresh ingredients for his recipes. He has started a list of items he needs. Uncle Ruff says he needs some things to fix the tiger trap as well.

"To town we go!" Uncle Ruff declares. "Lou, prepare yourself for the unbridled excitement that is the thriving metropolis of Corinna. Population: seventeen." He grins. "I'm joking of course, there's at least double that during happy hour at the pub."

On the drive to town, Colin becomes hyperfixated on the grocery list, reading the items over and over again.

"Don't worry, mate," Uncle Ruff tells him after a while. "You've got it covered."

Colin finally stops reading the list aloud but continues to study it silently.

After over an hour we reach the small township of Corinna and Uncle Ruff pulls up in front of a grocery store. "Jump out and get started," he says. "I'll get the supplies I need to fix the trap and I'll meet you back here to pay for the food."

The grocery store is tiny, about the size of an average convenience store back home. It's practically empty, save for a few seniors having a coffee in the front of the store.

"I have the list," Colin says unnecessarily, holding it aloft. He handles the list with military precision, barking out item after item. He insists on collecting the groceries in the order they're written, so we end up traveling back and forth through the aisles multiple times.

We're filling the cart with the remaining items from the produce section when I see two girls standing together, whispering, near the checkout counter. They look like the popular girls at my school. Pretty, with trendy clothes and shiny hair.

The girls glance at us, then whisper some more, until finally one pulls the other toward where we're standing.

"Hi, Colin," one says.

"We thought it was you," says the other.

The girls look at me eagerly. Clearly, they would like Colin to tell them who I am, but he is doing his best to ignore them. He is too focused on the grocery list to give them his attention. He's holding it up to his face in close scrutiny.

"Hi," I answer instead. "I'm Louisa. I'm visiting from Canada."

"Hi, how ya going?" they both reply in singsong unison.

"Canada! That's so awesome!" says one. "We never get to go anywhere." They giggle.

"I love your accent," says the other. "I'm Marisa, and this is Samantha."

I give a small, awkward wave.

"Are you staying at the Eco Lodge?" asks Samantha.

"No. I'm visiting my uncle who lives near there. He's friends with Colin's mom."

"Cool," says Samantha, but her sarcastic tone and smirk read the opposite.

Both girls look at Colin expectantly.

"How's your holidays going, Colin?" asks Marisa in a voice that sounds like she's talking to a small child. We all wait for Colin to reply. He still has the list awkwardly in front of his face. The cringeworthy moments drip by slowly and my stomach twists for him.

"My holidays are fine, thank you," he manages finally. "But

we don't have time to talk now because we still have five items left on the list." He looks around, unwilling to look at either girl. "To be accurate: apples, bananas, lemons, garlic, and parsley."

Both Marisa and Samantha snicker. "We just saw Mick and his mates at the footie oval. Don't you hang around with him anymore? You guys used to be best mates, right?"

Colin swallows. "No. I mean, yes. I don't know." He shifts from one foot to the other and taps his temple. "I—I have to go," he stammers before rushing to the fruit stand, out of earshot, where he begins to wrestle green apples into a plastic bag.

Marisa makes a face at Samantha. "He's so totally weird," she whispers.

"That's Colin," agrees Samantha. "Creepy." They giggle.

"No, he's not," I say.

Both girls look at me quizzically. "If you say so," says Marisa. "But he acts creepy and weird like that at school all the time." Her face takes on a false look of pity. "We were only trying to be nice by saying hi."

"Louisa," says Samantha, taking my arm conspiringly. "If you want to hang out, we could totally show you around and stuff. I'm sure you'd have a much better time with us. It must be a huge drag getting stuck with Colin for your holidays."

"No thanks," I say. "And, no. Actually. It's not a drag at all." I pull my arm away from her grasp. "I don't like your kind of 'nice.' Neither does Colin."

I push the cart away from them, my face flushed. Colin is now holding a bunch of bananas in each hand, in great indecision about which to buy. "Come on," I tell him, plucking one of the bunches from his hand and putting it in the cart. "Let's go. I see Uncle Ruff at the checkout."

"No!" Colin shouts loudly. "We still need lemons, garlic, and parsley!"

"Shhh. Chill out." I try to hush him. I'm mortified. For both of us. "You don't need to yell," I tell him from the side of my mouth.

I can see the girls giggling behind their hands.

"Here," I say, putting the final items in the cart. "Let's go."

Colin stops shouting but starts to flap his hands in front of his face. Something I've never see him do before. "Stop it," I say to him stupidly. I hate that I'm so embarrassed.

Uncle Ruff sees us. "Everything okay?" he asks, coming over to us.

I look back at Marisa and Samantha, who are now scanning magazine covers with expressions like Cheshire cats. "I guess," I say, feeling prickles of anger all over my skin.

Uncle Ruff sees the girls and nods slowly. "Gotcha." He watches Colin flapping his hands. "It's okay, mate," he says. "Let's get going."

We pay for and bag up the groceries and head back to the car. Colin is still flapping his hands around his face but follows us outside. I help Uncle Ruff load the bags into the trunk.

"It's just stimming," he tells me. "The flapping. It's nothing to worry about."

"Stimming?" I ask.

"It's a term for self-soothing. For when he's feeling overwhelmed or anxious. It helps him to calm down."

We finish loading the bags and I climb into the front seat of the jeep.

"Ready to go, mate?" Uncle Ruff asks Colin. "We're all set."

Colin spends a few minutes pacing around the jeep before he finally gets in the backseat. I notice that he has replaced the hand flapping with the more familiar temple tapping.

We're all quiet as we drive out of town. I watch out the window as we wind through the forest and my heartbeat settles back to normal. I'm trying to think of what to say to Colin. I feel bad for him, or for myself, I'm not sure, but he beats me to it.

"I'm sorry I shouted in the store," he says quietly. "I just… it's just…I don't like to be rushed."

"I'm sorry I tried to rush you," I say. "I'm sorry I upset you," I add. "I acted like a jerk."

I look in the mirror. Colin doesn't answer.

"Do you know those girls?" I ask him.

"I've seen them at high school," he says. "But I've never heard them say any of the mean things to me." He pauses. "I think they're okay."

"No, they're not," I say. Colin has always been honest with me, so the least I can do is be the same with him. "Just because they smile to your face doesn't mean they're being kind. Just because the *words* you hear aren't rude doesn't mean they're being nice. Stay away from them at school, okay? They're fakers."

Colin's eyes get stormy again. He wraps his arms protectively across his body and glares out the window, rocking. "That's why it's hard to make friends with new people," he says angrily. "I can't tell who I can trust." He remains silent the whole way home. I've upset him twice now, but I prefer that to him thinking Samantha and Marisa are nice.

I can feel Colin's pain and frustration. It brings up memories of my own that I'm not willing to think about, but they edge in anyway...of my last audition, sitting in the back of the car, frozen with anger and embarrassment. No matter how many times Mom asked what was wrong, I couldn't tell her.

I turn back to watching out the window to clear my thoughts. We pass along the long stretches of high roads through the mountains. I look down at the swaths of dense forest rushing by my window. Enormous trees, wild and rugged, as far as the eye can see, a sea of swaying green limbs. What secrets does this ancient forest harbor? I close my eyes and when I open them again, we're driving through a barren patch of land that has recently been logged. For all its vastness, the beauty is gone in the blink of an eye.

When we pull up at the camp, another car is parked close to Uncle Ruff's cabin. The sedan has an official-looking logo on the side. Two men are standing near the car; one is smoking a cigarette.

Uncle Ruff sighs. "This can't be good," he says. "You kids unload the bags and I'll deal with these guys." He gets out of the car.

"Hello there, gentlemen," Ruff says in a loud, confident voice, walking toward them. "What can I do for you?"

The men extend their hands to one another and all shake amicably.

"Who are they?" I ask Colin.

"They're from the city council," says Colin, his first words in an hour. He's leaning forward to get a look at what's going on. "Mum calls them *government red-tapers in their unnatural habitat.*"

I chuckle. I'm relieved that Colin is talking again, although he still has a haunted expression.

"Come on," I say. "Let's unload the groceries."

We carry the bags from the jeep into the kitchen, making more trips than necessary so we can try to eavesdrop, but the city men and Uncle Ruff have taken their conversation to the river's edge where we can't hear them. Half an hour goes by before Uncle Ruff comes into the cabin. He holds some papers in his hands and sits heavily on a chair at the kitchen table.

"We're being evicted," he says.

15

Devil Rescue

I put away the groceries and Colin goes on the short-wave radio to tell Mel about the visit from the city men and the impending eviction. She promises to come right over.

Uncle Ruff pounds away at his laptop, doing what, we're not sure.

When Mel arrives she's carrying a laundry basket, but this time it isn't full of food, it looks to have bundles of towels inside. She plonks the basket on the kitchen table. "Say hello to your new friends," she says.

We peer into the basket as two wet noses poke out. I slap a hand over my mouth to stifle a scream. A pair of pink-eared, black-furred, pup-sized creatures tumble and claw over one another.

"Devil joeys," says Colin.

"What happened?" asks Uncle Ruff, reaching in and picking up the baby devils, one in each large hand. He looks them over. "A boy and a girl. Seem pretty healthy," he adds.

"Their mum was hit by a car. Some hikers dropped them at the Eco Lodge before I left. By the looks of them, they're lucky. I don't see any injuries." Mel gives them a pet. "I hoped you'd be able to take care of them until I can get them to the devil sanctuary at Cradle Mountain."

Uncle Ruff peers at each joey. "At this age they've left the pouch but stay close to mum. Likely they were watching Mum cross the road and waiting until it was safe to follow." He puts one back in the basket and gives the other a more thorough examination. "I'd say they're around three months old." Uncle Ruff turns the joey so they're face-to-face. "I bet you and your sister are hungry, huh?" He hands me the devil. "Hold him while I get some bottles and milk."

I gasp as the devil joey squirms in my grasp. He's in constant motion, clawing and scratching at my sweater, trying to crawl up to my shoulders. I can't help but giggle as he burrows his nose in my hair, sniffing. His thick black fur is very soft. Colin picks up the other one. The girl. He dangles her, his arms outstretched, looking into her face as her little legs cycle in the air.

"You look like a Matilda," Colin says.

Mel laughs. "Then this one will have to be Waltz," she says, giving my charge a scratch on the head.

"Oh, I get it," says Colin. "Waltz and Matilda."

"Isn't that a song?" I ask. "I read about it in Eleanor's journal."

"'Waltzing Matilda' is the unofficial Australian anthem. It's the story of a wandering bushman in the outback who steals a sheep, and rather than getting captured by the law, he jumps into a waterhole to his death."

"Wow. Talk about intense," I say, peeling the joey from the top of my head.

"Oh, the tune itself is quite upbeat," says Mel. "Aussies love a rebel story. Originally it was a protest song against wealthy landowners and their treatment of the workers. It was a rally cry for social justice."

Uncle Ruff reappears with two baby bottles filled with what I assume is milk. He takes Waltz and wraps him in a towel, just like swaddling a baby. Then he settles him back in my arms, handing me the bottle. "If you wrap 'em up like that, it keeps their claws out of the way." He helps me angle the bottle into the joey's mouth and Waltz starts drinking greedily. I giggle, watching Waltz lap at the milk and blink his dark marble eyes. He watches me trustingly. Except for his long tail, he reminds me of a black bear cub. Uncle Ruff hums a tune as he feeds Waltz's sister. I'm guessing the tune is "Waltzing Matilda." Mel and Colin join in and they sing the whole song. When it's finished, I ask Colin, "What's a billabong?"

"A waterhole," he replies. "Most likely a large dam or a river."

"And a billy?"

"A tin can," says Colin. "To boil water to make tea."

"And a jumbuck?"

"A sheep."

"So, the story goes," I say, recalling the lyrics, "a swagman, or a drifter, is hanging out at a billabong making tea when a sheep comes along and he catches it. Then the police show up and accuse him of stealing, so he jumps into the water and drowns rather than going to jail...and then his ghost haunts the billabong?"

"That is a correct summary of the story, yes." says Colin. "The phrase 'Waltzing' was slang at the time for traveling by foot and 'Matilda' is what the swagmen called their blanket roll."

The tune itself is catchy and now I have it in my head. I can't help but hum it to myself.

With their bellies full, the babies are serenaded off to sleep. We all smile at one another, looking at the peaceful faces of the sleeping joeys. I carefully place Waltz, still wrapped up in the towel, back in the basket. Ruff does the same with Matilda. He puts the basket gently on the floor and we sit at the kitchen table to drink the tea Colin has brewed. With the joeys settled for now, our thoughts return to our impending eviction from the camp.

"Isn't there something we can do?" I ask. "Can't we just refuse to leave?"

"Sure," says Mel. "We can protest, we can call every media outlet in Australia and chain ourselves to the trees—believe me, I have done all of those things in the past to try and stop logging and mining from destroying the Tarkine—but it will bring the world to our door, and we can't risk that happening."

"Mum was a Tarkine tiger," says Colin. "She protested

against the original road being built into the Tarkine back in the '90s. She even got arrested," he adds with a hint of pride.

"That was a long time ago," Mel says. "Now my energy goes into conservation and educating visitors instead." She winks at Colin. "And a few other things keep me busy besides."

"I'm sorry, Lou," says Uncle Ruff. "The bridge construction wasn't meant to start until months from now. But apparently the mild winter conditions have ramped up their plans. If we'd known it was going to start so soon, I would have told your mum not to send you."

I'm silent. The idea of never having come here—of never having had the chance to meet Mel, Colin, Piggy, or Uncle Ruff, of never learning about Eleanor, Shadow, Freddie, and Old Stevie—of not ever holding a Tasmanian devil joey: it all seems unthinkable.

"But if we tell people about Ellie and the other tigers," I insist, "surely they won't bulldoze the camp to build the road or dynamite Convict Rock for the bridge." I know I'm stating the obvious but I can't help it. "Can't we try?"

"No. That is not what Eleanor wanted. We promised her," Uncle Ruff replies. "I promised her. And it's not what I want either. It would end up causing even more of the Tarkine to be destroyed. And Ellie would die in captivity." Uncle Ruff shakes his head. "No. The only thing we can do is try to trap her so she can be moved to safety. This camp and Convict Rock have given all they can. It's not safe here for Ellie anymore, or for any other tigers either. And with Piggy gone, there's no point in me staying here. My work is done."

"How long do we have?" Mel asks.

"Two weeks," says Ruff. "That's if they keep their word. We're here on borrowed time. The men came as a courtesy so we can clear out our belongings. But they have the permits to start anytime they like."

"Two weeks isn't very long," says Colin.

"Nope," says Uncle Ruff. "We'd better get cracking on that trap, mate."

"But what if we can't catch her?" Colin asks.

We all look at one another. We don't speak. No one wants to imagine it—the camp being bulldozed, Convict Rock being dynamited, and Ellie exposed and alone, her habitat destroyed.

I look at the devil joeys, so small and vulnerable, sleeping in the laundry basket at our feet.

"We have to do everything we can," I say. "We have to try."

I need some fresh air so I take my violin and walk the path that I first arrived on. I want to see the forest in the same way that Eleanor wrote about it in her journal. I wander the trail and try to see through her eyes. I search for the ruby-red toadstools and scan the forest floor for fallen trunks like the ones she used as a pretend piano. I don't see any red mushrooms or hollowed-out logs, but for the first time I notice other things. Towering eucalypts sway above me in a canopy of dappled grays, blues, and greens, fanning out a scent of lemon myrtle and tea tree. A delicate moss hangs over spindly saplings in the undergrowth. The moss is like a lace shawl forgotten on the forest floor.

I sit on a mossy stump that is surprisingly dry and soft. I

close my eyes and hear the birdsong again, Vivaldi's "Spring." I lift the violin to my chin to begin my usual audition pieces, but "Waltzing Matilda" still rings in my head. I guess the chords and begin to play the ballad by ear.

And for the first time since I arrived, I don't hear false notes, I just hear music.

The afternoon evaporates as I play, wrapped up in the gums, moss, and leaves. After a time, I put my instrument down and realize dusk has settled in. The currawong birds have ceased their song and the bush is beginning to turn shadowy and dim. I stand up and stretch. I need to get back to the camp before the sun sets. I don't want a repeat of getting lost in the dark.

As I put my violin in its case, I hear the unmistakable sound of something large moving through the undergrowth, near where I'm standing. I hold my breath and it stops. My mind races at what it could be: devils, possums, pademelon, wallabies? I see the tops of the fern fronds a few yards away swaying, disturbed by something underneath. I hear the crackling of twigs and the swish of branches again, this time closer to me. I want to run but I'm frozen to the spot. Do I shout for help, hoping one of the others will hear me?

Then I hear another sound, the short, rhythmic panting again. Then a high-pitched *cough, cough, yip, yip*. The same sounds I heard on my first night at the camp.

In a lightning flash, I see two huge dark eyes blinking at me from under the ferns.

16

Voices

I run back to the camp and burst into the cabin. Mel and Colin are in the kitchen preparing dinner and Uncle Ruff is holding the eviction paperwork close to his face, frowning at it. The devil joeys are asleep in the basket, now positioned near the fire.

"She's here!" I shout breathlessly.

"Who?" asks Ruff, glancing up from his paperwork.

"Ellie!" I say, and I tell them what happened.

Uncle Ruff scratches his beard. "But what did you actually *see*?" he asks.

"It was a flash, like seconds, but I'm certain. Two large dark eyes under the ferns. And I could hear her too, moving in the undergrowth," I insist.

"But it could have been another animal, right?" he asks gently.

"As much as we'd like to conjure her up," adds Mel, "we have to think realistically. We are all a bit panicky right now."

"But I heard her too." I describe the *cough, cough, yip, yip* sound and Uncle Ruff's face looks suddenly astonished. Now I have his attention. "And listen," I go on. "Remember the first night? When I woke up to that funky smell? I heard the same noise that night too. I had been playing violin then as well, and it had gotten dark. She must have come to listen. Tonight's the only other time I've played at dusk."

"Okay, I'm not saying you're wrong," says Mel. "It's just... well, it's likely wishful thinking, hon. I mean, we've just been talking about her. We all want to find her."

Uncle Ruff has started to pace around the cabin.

"Hang on a minute," he says. "Lou might be on to something. The vocalization she described is spot-on. That first night, when Lou was playing, if Ellie was drawn to the music for some reason, it would explain why she emitted her defensive odor. Because when she got close to Lou's cabin to hear the music, she detected a new human scent—which, for her, could equal danger." He pauses. "Tonight she was drawn to the music again, but she's familiar with Lou's scent now and didn't feel threatened." He stops. "And what if Lou's violin somehow mimics the notes of a tiger's vocalization? Ellie is alone, so she is desperate to find other tigers at this point. She could be drawn to the sound of Lou's violin so strongly because she thinks the violin is another tiger calling her."

"Or maybe she just has good taste in music," says Colin earnestly, which makes me smile.

"She was likely very young when the pack left," Uncle Ruff continues. "So she isn't familiar with tiger language. She's just going on instinct."

"And hope," adds Mel. "She probably wants to find other tigers as much as we want to find her."

Uncle Ruff goes to his bedroom and rummages around. He comes out ten minutes later with a small black object held high above his head.

"What's that?" asks Colin.

"This," says Ruff, "is tiger bait."

"Bait? It looks like an old tape recorder," I say.

"It is. You're going to play us a concert, Lou." He taps the recorder. "And then we'll set up the recorder to play back your music inside the trap."

"Clever," says Mel.

"No. It's Lou here who's the clever one." He winks at me. "Our very own tiger whisperer, a chip off old Eleanor's block."

I feel a flush of pride down to my toes.

"It's a long shot, but it's all we've got. Tomorrow, me and Colin will fix the trap and Lou will record her masterpiece." He places the recorder on the table. "Tomorrow night we'll be ready for Ellie."

The devil joeys pull our attention away from Ellie's capture. Waltz and Matilda have woken up, climbed out of the laundry hamper, and are trotting around the cabin, climbing everything in their path.

"Let's put them in Piggy's old pen," says Uncle Ruff. "I'll mix up some more formula for them first. Artificial milk will be fine for them for the next while until we get them to the sanctuary." It's good to see Uncle Ruff in his element again, taking care of wildlife.

Colin and I scurry after the joeys but they are too fast. It becomes a game of hide-and-seek for them, on and around the sofa, on and under the kitchen table. By the time we've corralled both devils we're out of breath. I hold Waltz above my head. "I got you now, you little rascal, you," I say, stroking his silky fur. It's jet-black except for a white spot on his rump. Matilda is fully black, so it's easy to tell them apart. Colin cradles Matilda gently in his arms. "Soft," he murmurs, rubbing Matilda's fur on his cheek.

We wrap them up and feed them, like Uncle Ruff showed us. They don't fall asleep this time. "It's dark now," says Ruff. "Devils are mostly nocturnal. These babies will be partying all night, most likely."

I place Waltz in the pen. He clings to my hand with his front claws. "Go on," I say, nudging him away. "I'll see you in the morning," I promise him.

Back in my cabin, it's hard to sleep from the excitement of our plan. I am tempted to play my violin, but I promised everyone I'd save my fingers to record a full practice set tomorrow.

I close my eyes, listening to the night music of the ancient bush around me. I hear the trees creaking and the throaty murmuring of frogs. The hypnotic forest symphony eventually lulls me to sleep and I dream of tiger eyes staring out at me from the dark.

17

Cabin Visitor

The next morning, Mel wakes me up with a mug of tea.

"I wanted to say goodbye before I head back to the Eco Lodge," she says, sitting on the edge of the bed. "And to say thank you."

I sit up and take the steaming tea from her. "For what?"

"For being Colin's friend. For being there for him yesterday."

"Oh. I don't know if I was much of a friend. I mean, I upset him. I tried to rush him out of the store. I shouldn't have." I take a sip of tea. "I like Colin. Honestly. It's been good having him here. I'm not just saying it to be polite, I mean it."

"You were there for him and you were honest with him. In my books, that's being a friend." Mel looks at me with her kind eyes. "The scene with the girls couldn't have been comfortable for you, either."

"Did Colin talk to you about yesterday?" I ask.

"Yes. We discussed it. Practicing social scenarios is something we've tried to work on. In the past we've role-played and written scripts, but I guess the interaction yesterday took him by surprise. He'll need to return to school soon and having made a new friend, with you, gives him real confidence. Now that he knows he can do it, he just needs to do it at school." She pats my knee. "And sooner or later someone like you will look past his quirks and want to get to know him."

"They weren't very nice, those girls," I say. "But he couldn't tell."

"It's difficult for him to pick up on nonverbal social cues. Especially with girls." She chuckles. "I think they make him especially nervous. Which is probably true for most boys his age."

I take another sip of the tea. Mel has given me an idea.

"They just don't understand yet," she continues. "When people don't understand something, they tend to generalize and use labels, like 'weird.' I aim to change that. There is a need to educate about the acceptance of neurodiversity."

"Neurodiversity?" I ask.

"Neurodiversity means the variety we all have regarding social skills, learning abilities, attention spans, moods." She grins. "We are all different, that's all."

"I've noticed," I say.

"Well, you're one of us now," she says, getting up from the mattress. "Whether you like it or not."

"Mel?" I call out as she's leaving. She stops and turns. "Can you e-mail my mom for me?" I ask. "Let her know that...that I miss her. And that I love her?"

"Of course," says Mel with a gentle smile. "I'd be happy to."

Mel leaves and I go to Uncle Ruff's cabin. I open the screen porch and peek into the devil pen. Both joeys are fast asleep, so I go into the cabin. Breakfast is bacon and farm-fresh eggs. There's an air of excitement in the kitchen. "Come in and eat up, Lou!" orders Uncle Ruff. "You have a tiger concert to perform." He piles my plate with scrambled eggs and rashes of bacon. "Did you sleep well?" he asks. "How are those violin pluckers of yours today, hm?"

"Good, thanks," I answer. "Did you get any sleep?" I ask him. "Did the joeys keep you up?"

"Nah," he says, but I suspect they did. "Let's get down to business," he says, chomping on a piece of toast. "Where should we record, do you reckon?" he asks me.

"My cabin has good acoustics, actually," I say. "I'll record in there."

"Excellent," says Uncle Ruff. "I've put new batteries in the machine." He pats the recorder where it still sits on the table from last night. "All you need to do is press this button when you're ready to record." He points to the record button and takes a sip of tea. "And this one to stop. Or you can just let the tape run out, no worries."

"Got it," I say.

"Me and Colin will get cracking on the trap repairs. Right, mate?" He looks at Colin.

"Affirmative," says Colin, settling into a chair to eat his breakfast.

"How will the trap work, exactly?" I ask.

"It's a standard humane animal trap," replies Uncle Ruff. "Just like you'd use to catch a raccoon or skunk back in Toronto. Just bigger," he adds.

"There's a collapsible flap to enter the trap that closes behind the animal so they can't get out," Colin explains further. "Usually the trap is baited with food, but we're going put your music inside instead."

"Have you tried with food?" I ask.

"Oh, yes indeed," says Uncle Ruff. "And I've caught many, many possums. It's been an all-night bush diner."

"Time to change tactics," adds Colin.

"That's where I come in," I say, pleased to be a part of the plan.

"Exactly," says Uncle Ruff. "Just play as you have been." He peers at me. "No need to be nervous," he adds.

"I'm not nervous," I say unconvincingly.

"Don't worry about any bad notes," he goes on. "It could be out-of-tune notes that attract Ellie, for all we know."

"I hadn't thought of that," I say.

He taps his nose. "I'm not just a pretty face with a beard, you know."

"You also can't tell the difference," I say. "You're tone-deaf. Musical notes all sound the same to you."

"Well, yes," he admits. "There's that too."

I finish eating and gather up the recorder to take back to my cabin.

"Try not to get any human sounds on the tape, like coughing or sneezing. No talking, obviously." He stops. "Do you want an audience?" he asks.

"Definitely not," I say. "But thanks anyway."

I go to my cabin and settle down on the wooden chair. I place the recorder close by on the edge of the bed, and take my violin out of its case. I press the record button and then pick up my bow and raise the instrument to my chin.

As I begin to play I see something move in the corner of the cabin, near the top of the doorframe. A large creature with long hairy legs, but I don't scream.

"I guess it's going to rain again, huh?" I ask her.

The spider settles herself on the wooden beam.

I take a deep breath. "All right," I tell her. "I guess you can stay this time."

As I raise my bow, I can't help but smile to myself. Never in my wildest dreams when I left Toronto could I have imagined that I'd be recording a practice session in the hopes of attracting an extinct marsupial called Ellie, with a huntsman spider for an audience.

I hardly recognize myself. And I like it.

18

Time Is Running Out

Things aren't going to plan. It's been a week since Uncle Ruff set the tiger trap with the recording of my music. He's tried setting the recorder inside the trap, beside the trap, and on top of the trap. No Ellie. He also set up a motion-sensitive camera to try to capture her on film, but she has eluded us, and the camera. Every morning on the discovery of the empty trap—and after watching camera footage of curious pademelon and pushy possums—we discuss new strategies over breakfast.

"The recorded music clearly isn't providing the same lure as your live music did," reasoned Uncle Ruff. "It could be something to do with static or feedback in the recording. Frequencies that are undetectable to us could be piercing to her."

"I could play live, like I did the other times," I say. I'm sitting by the woodstove with a snoozy Waltz and Matilda in my lap. The weather has become much colder in the last few days. It's lovely to cuddle up with the babies, who are fast becoming grown. Although Uncle Ruff is quick to remind me that they are not pets.

Mel and Uncle Ruff have been too busy to take them to the devil sanctuary yet, which is hours away, but I suspect Uncle Ruff enjoys having Piggy's pen occupied again.

"Yes, you could play live," agreed Uncle Ruff. "But how is that going to coax her into the trap? Food hasn't worked." He thinks some more. "Plus, I really believe human scent, so close to the trap, will put her off."

"Maybe we have to rethink the trap," says Colin. "How else could she be captured?"

"Actually," says Uncle Ruff, "back in the old days, Eleanor asked Old Stevie to help her catch one of Shadow's pups because she had spotted what looked like mange. She was worried that it would infect the rest of the pack. Those were the days before humane traps. The only traps back then were metal jaws that broke the leg of the animal."

"Is that how Old Stevie caught Shadow's mother?" I asked.

"Sadly, yes," says Uncle Ruff. "So obviously she wasn't going to use his old hunting traps."

I shivered at the thought of it.

"Anyway, Old Stevie made a net," Uncle Ruff goes on. "That's what Eleanor told me. But in those days, the tigers were crossing from here to Convict Rock regularly and they knew when and where the pack would drink at the river. And that pack were used to humans and didn't bolt at the sight or scent of us." He looks out of the window. "That was the last time a tiger was handled by a human here at the camp. Eleanor realized that she couldn't let the tigers get so used to people. From then on, she purely observed them, and that's what she taught us too. Not to interfere, just to observe and allow the tigers to have Convict Rock as a refuge, as needed." He stops to think. "Eleanor had good instincts. I've since read accounts, from back in the bounty-hunting days, of the tigers being very timid, not in the least aggressive. They were captured without a fight and would often die suddenly, perhaps from going into shock."

"Did the pup have mange?" I asked.

"He did. Eleanor treated it with vinegar, if you can believe it, and sent it back to his family. But it troubled her that it was so easy for them to catch and handle the pup."

"So we make a net," says Colin. "Or what about a lasso pole, like you see animal rescuers use on television? A long pole with a loop at the end to put over her head."

Uncle Ruff nods slowly. "Sure, mate, we can try. Let's give it a shot. But to use either a net or a noose would mean having Ellie close enough to catch. It would mean being in arm's length of a tiger." He pauses. "In all of my years here, the only sightings I've ever had have been at a distance, or on camera, or by secondary evidence. Never close up." Uncle Ruff looks at us both. "We also have to consider the fact that she just isn't here anymore. At this point we are only going on Lou's hunch. I've seen no tracks, or scat, or signs of her hunting. She might have moved on of her own accord."

"But you said she might be injured," I say. "That's why the pack left her. It isn't likely that she would leave by herself, is it? What if she's hurt over on Convict Rock and can't swim over?"

"One thing is for sure," he says. "We better hurry up and catch her. If she's still here. Time is running out. It's one week before the place gets 'dozed and dynamited." His tone is upbeat but I can see the masked worry on his face.

Colin and Uncle Ruff go outside and get to work on the net and the lasso. I put the devil joeys back in the pen and finish the breakfast dishes. I pick up a book that is lying on the kitchen counter. It's a well-worn paperback about Tasmanian tigers. It occurs to me that I really don't know very much about this mysterious animal, only what I've read in Eleanor's journal and what the others have told me. I sit at the kitchen counter and start reading.

Thylacines, commonly known as Tasmanian tigers, are doglike, carnivorous marsupials. They are known as shy, nocturnal creatures that carry their young in pouches, like kangaroos. Even the male tigers have a pouch. They are sandy brown or gray in color and sport dark, tigerlike stripes on their backs. Their tails are long and stiff and they have an impressively wide and powerful jaw. Female tigers are significantly smaller than males. A litter consists of up to four young with the mother caring for the young

until they are half grown. The tigers are not known to run at great speeds but rather lope with a stiff gait. Observations have been made of the animal hopping on its back legs. Reports were also made of the tiger giving off an odor when agitated.

The animal was once found all across Australia and New Guinea. Fossils of early tigers have been unearthed in parts of Australia that date from about thirty million to twelve million years ago. Modern tigers vanished from the mainland of Australia about three thousand years ago, probably from a combination of a drying climate and competition with the Australian wild dog, the dingo. The tiger kept a foothold on the island state of Tasmania, where there is no dingo population, long after it vanished from the mainland. The tigers continued to roam Tasmania for thousands of years before European settlers arrived in the 1800s. At that time the European settlers perceived the tigers as a threat to their livestock and created a cash bounty for their pelts. The last Tasmanian tiger, known as Benjamin, died in the Hobart Zoo in 1936.

I put down the book, remembering Eleanor's account of visiting Benjamin in the Hobart Zoo with her grandmother, also remembering the grainy black-and-white film Colin showed me. And here I was, all these years later, trying to help Ellie.

I leave the cabin and walk to the river's edge, to where Uncle Ruff and Colin are working on their tiger-catching devices. Colin holds a fishing pole with a net at the end. He is cutting off the netting so the end of the pole has a bare metal loop. Uncle Ruff is stitching burlap sacks together.

"We have to go to Convict Rock," I tell them.

19

Bushwalk

Uncle Ruff stands up and looks over the river to the imposing rocky island. He takes a deep breath. "I think you might be right," he says. "It could be our only chance to find her. But I'm going to need time to gather stuff to take over."

We all agree to be ready before dusk to make the trip over to Convict Rock.

"We have time to kill," I say to Colin. "Take me on one of your famous bushwalks."

"I'm not sure 'famous' is totally accurate, but I'm rated highly on TripAdvisor," he says. "I have forty-three five-star ratings, to be exact."

"Good enough for me," I say. "Bring your phone," I add as we head out.

"Why? There isn't cell range here," he says.

"Just bring it anyway," I say.

Colin puts his phone, together with a canteen of water, mosquito repellent, a first-aid kit, energy bars, a flashlight, matches, and a blanket into his backpack.

"We're not going to stay out all day and all night," I say.

"Best to be prepared," says Colin. "We'll take the old hunting trail."

After we've walked for a few minutes, Colin begins his five-star guided tour.

"The Tarkine forest is the largest tract of temperate rain forest in the southern hemisphere," he says, "and it's the natural habitat for over fifty threatened species, including the wedge-tailed eagle and the eastern barred bandicoot. Stands of Huon pine here have been found to date back ten thousand years and the Tasmanian tiger had roamed the region for thousands of years."

An enveloping dampness creeps in as we walk deeper down the forest path. The hunting track Colin has chosen runs along a babbling stream. An early rain has left the leaves glistening with moisture. Boulders and rocks are encased in silvery lichens. Up ahead, a massive tree trunk appears to be suspended in midair. The fallen limb, dripping with lacy greenery, is cradled between the branches of a giant blue gum and looms above us like a sacred gateway. The setting is ancient and mysterious, a feeling heightened by knowing that the forest has stood here for millions of years.

I rest my hand on the scaly, brown, spiraling trunk of an enormous tree. "What do you call this guy?" I ask, looking upward to its towering canopy of small, ivy-shaped leaves.

"Myrtle," says Colin. "Also known as myrtle beech. The basalt soil here gives the wood a red to pinkish hue. It makes the wood highly sought after. It has a tiny white flower in spring."

"And that one?" I ask, pointing to the narrow gray trunk of a smaller tree.

"That's a blackwood. From the acacia species, also commonly called black wattle, hickory, or mudgerabah. Known for its densely packed, sphere-shaped flowers that range from white to gold in color, typical of the wattle family."

"How did you learn so much about the bush?" I ask.

"The Tarkine is one of my special-interest subjects. I read a lot about the forest and take notes in my journal. I can usually answer any questions the hikers at the Eco Lodge have." He waves his hand around. "It's surprising how little people see in nature until you point it out to them. Native laurel, leatherwood, Antarctic beech trees: there is a wide array of biodiversity here. The forest is nourished by approximately three metres of rainfall per year." He kneels at the stream. "In summer, giant freshwater crayfish are found in the area." He dips his hand into the trickling water. "It's too cold now though." He stands and shakes the water from his hand. "The crayfish, an invertebrate, is endangered, so it is not permitted to catch one. They can live up to sixty years and become as large as a small dog." Colin indicates the size with his hands before we keep walking. "Tasmania has three species of snake and they're all venomous," Colin offers. "The white-lipped, the lowland copperhead, and the tiger snake. The white-lipped is small so its fangs can't cause too much harm, but the tiger and the copperhead are large, so hikers should proceed with extreme caution if a sighting occurs. We always recommend hikers include bandages with their provisions in case they are bitten. Bandaging the area largely increases the chance of survival."

"But...there aren't any snakes around here now...are there?" I ask hesitantly.

"Oh definitely, there are," says Colin. "But they are generally inactive in the winter months. They usually retreat into rodent burrows, hollow logs, or tree stumps." Colin stops to think. "Although it's not unknown for them to come out when the winter is mild."

I move closer to Colin and grip his sleeve. "Are they easy to see?" I ask, looking from left to right of the track.

"No. To be accurate, they are usually extremely well camouflaged. Most bites occur because a hiker steps on one by accident."

I grip Colin's sleeve tighter. Every twisted tree root suddenly looks like a snake.

"Are you scared?" Colin asks, looking at my hand gripping his sleeve.

"Of course I'm scared."

"There really is no need to be scared. Despite their ability to blend in to the environment, I am quite experienced at spotting snakes. Given the opportunity, snakes will retreat of their own accord. In my entire experience of bushwalking, I have never been bitten, so there is a very high statistical chance that you will not get bitten either—because you're with me."

I shiver, remembering walking out on my own and sitting on tree stumps.

"Uncle Ruff told me not to worry because it's winter," I say miserably.

"He is right. Generally speaking. For the most part. Statistically around 80 percent."

"Sometimes I wish you could just lie a little. You know...to make me feel better."

"Oh. Okay." Colin straightens up. "There is absolutely zero chance you will get bitten by a snake and die today."

"Thank you."

We continue along the track until we reach a clearing. The sun makes a welcome appearance. A blush of warmth brushes our faces. I scan the clearing for snakes but don't see anything.

"Stop here a minute," I say to Colin.

He looks around the clearing. "Would you like to take a break?" he asks.

"Yes. No. It's not that. I wanted to do something."

"What?" asks Colin.

"Remember those girls we saw in Corinna?" I ask.

"Yes. Marisa and Samantha. From school. The *fakers*, you called them."

"Right. You couldn't tell they were being mean. I'm going to show you how you can tell. At least until you get to know everyone better. Get out your phone."

I smile at Colin. "This is a normal smile," I say. "Take a photo and put a caption saying *Nice*."

I smirk. "This is a smile when I'm being sarcastic. Can you see a difference?"

"Yes," Colin replies. "The shape of your lips is different. One side goes up."

I roll my eyes. "This is what girls do when they're being mean without actually saying anything mean."

Colin keeps taking my photo and adding captions.

"And before you talk to someone, try taking a step back," I say, stepping an arm's length away. "About here is right."

Colin looks at the ground, mentally gauging the distance.

"And another thing. If two girls are talking to you and then start whispering to each other, that's rude." I mimic whispering conspiringly. "Obviously everyone's expressions will be different, but you can pretty much guarantee whispering isn't nice."

Then I speak in a singsong voice like the girls did. "If someone is talking to you like that, like you're a little kid, they're talking down to you. And another thing," I say. "Listen to what they're saying. Why would they ask you about Mick like that? There's no reason other than to make you feel bad." I search Colin's face to see if he gets what I'm saying.

"Do you understand?" I ask.

"Yes, I do. This is very helpful, Louisa, thank you."

Colin holds the phone up again. "Hold still," he says, his voice calm and quiet. "Very still."

"What is it? Is it a snake?" I whisper, panic gripping me.

"Don't move," he says.

20

The Pieman

I freeze on the spot. "Please, make it go away," I whisper.

"*Terror*," says Colin, tapping his phone.

"What?"

"I just wanted to capture a look of true terror. I'm calling it *Scared of snakes*."

"Wait. So there's no snake?"

A smile breaks out on Colin's usually anxious face. "No," he says.

I whip around to see for myself. There is no snake. I pick up a handful of dirt and throw it at him, but it doesn't even get close. The dirt blows in my face instead, making me cough. My coughing fit turns into laughter.

"I made a joke," he says. "Was it a good one? Is that why you're laughing?" Colin studies my reaction.

"Yes...yes, it was." I hiccup. "You got me."

And for the first time, I'm treated to Colin's raucous, infectious laughter.

We make our way back to the camp but still have hours until Uncle Ruff will take us to Convict Rock, so Colin suggests we go out in the skiff to catch trout.

We drop anchor close to shore and cast our lines, cracking the silvery surface of the water. We've been bobbing around for some time without a single nibble.

"It's the wrong time of day to expect to catch anything," says Colin. "The optimal time to catch fish is early morning or early evening."

"It's nice to be out here anyway," I say, dragging my hand through the cold, glowing water. "I didn't know I liked fishing so much."

"To be accurate, it's not fishing if you don't catch anything," Colin states.

"Whatever it is, I like it. It feels like you're doing something when you're just sitting here, doing nothing." It's not like me to be happy doing nothing. It's not like me to be happy without a violin in my hands.

Colin leans back in the boat. "I prefer it to school, that's for sure."

"You don't like school?" I ask.

Colin whips his fishing rod up and recasts the line. "Yes," he says finally. "I do. I like school. I know it will get easier once I find some friends." He flicks his rod again.

I watch the water as tiny bubbles surface. Maybe a slippery frog is watching us from below.

"You're brave," I say.

"How do you mean?"

"You talk about your challenges," I say. "You ask for help."

"It doesn't mean I always get the right answers."

"But it helps," I insist.

"Yes, it does," he admits.

"There's something I haven't told you," I begin. "Well, I haven't told anyone, really." I keep my eyes on the bubbles, finding it easier to speak to the hidden frog. "The reason I haven't gotten into the youth symphony orchestra is because I can't handle the auditions." I trip my fingers over the bubbles, making them disappear. "I totally freak out," I go on. "Nerves grip me until I'm totally paralyzed. I can't play even a single note."

I watch a snatch of my reflection on the river's surface. A blurry, moving shape.

"Hm," he says after a while. "I never would have guessed that you have performance anxiety. You seem to be completely neurotypical."

"What is neurotypical?"

"Normal."

"It's just when it comes to performing solo, when I'm being judged, something physical takes over," I say, turning to face him. "I feel normal until it comes to auditioning, then I freeze. I can barely breathe." I look back at the water. "I'm okay playing in a group, but if I'm singled out, or have to play solo in front of anyone, all I can think about is being criticized. Of not being good enough. Of making a fool of myself." I glance at Colin. "This isn't good for someone who wants to be a classical musician one day," I add.

"Have you told your parents?" asks Colin.

"No. I guess they know I've been stressed about the audition. But they don't know I haven't been able to perform at auditions. I just tell them it didn't go well." I flick my fishing line and it trembles before settling again. "It never used to be a problem until last year when I froze during a school concert. It was awful. I was so embarrassed." I shudder, remembering the horrible moments of silence as the entire school population had waited, and waited, for my solo. In the end, the music teacher had pointed to Alicia, who stood up and effortlessly performed my piece. I had sat down, wishing I could disappear, sick to my stomach. I've been haunted by the humiliation ever since. "At the time, I thought it was because I hadn't prepared properly," I tell Colin. "If I had just practiced more. If I was perfect. I wouldn't freeze up. But it keeps happening." I nudge my knee against his. "At least you talk to your mum about how you feel," I say. "I'm even too scared to do that much."

"But you are brave," says Colin.

"I don't see how," I say.

"Because you keep trying," he says. "Doing something despite being afraid is the definition of bravery."

"Well, we sure are some pair," I say.

"And we're bad at fishing too," says Colin.

It feels good to sit together in the small boat. We keep our lines in the water, not catching fish. Talking and not talking. The sun is beginning to throw a shadow over Convict Rock, where we'll try to catch Ellie. If she's still there.

"Tell me about the convicts on Convict Rock," I say to Colin. "The ghost stories."

"Okay. I know how to tell the story quite well," he says. "It is included in my five-star TripAdvisor tour." Colin eases himself into a comfortable position and props his rod against his leg. "Back when Tasmania was a convict settlement—" he begins.

"It was called Van Diemen's Land," I interrupt.

"Correct," he says. "The prison conditions were harsh and brutal, but Sarah Island, a small island downriver from here in Macquarie Harbour, was the worst of them all. That's where they sent the hardened criminals. The convicts lived in terrible conditions and were worked extremely hard, felling huon pine to build boats. There was a reason the law chose Sarah Island. It's remote, it still is. Any prisoners trying to escape not only had to cross the harbor, but they were in the wildest, most dense bush. No civilization for days and days."

I look at the tree line looming over the river. Conical spears of sassafras dot the heavy cover of gums and myrtle. It's not hard to imagine, without roads and cars, how impenetrable this land would be.

"So, the story goes, four convicts ran away while they were logging deep in the forest. They didn't have any supplies, just the day's rations of tea and damper, a kind of bread, and no warm clothes for the cold nights. Not even proper shoes." Colin quickly checks to see if I'm still listening. "One of the men, they called him the pieman, because he'd been a baker once, he was the only man to carry a weapon. It was a rough handsaw used to mark the tree trunks that were to be felled. The escape was hard work. The forest was thick with mosquitoes and snakes, plus the hunger was so brutal that after a week of bushwhacking one of the convicts said, 'Prison is better than this!' He wanted to turn back. It started troubles among the men. The pieman didn't want anyone going back, he feared it would lead the law to their gang. He threatened death to anyone who wanted to leave. And then he says, 'And if we have to kill ya, we may as well hack ya up and eat ya afterwards.'" I smile at the accent Colin attempts for the convicts. "The men were so starved that they feared he meant it. Worse still, they feared they'd become such savages that they'd go along with it. No one could sleep for fear of being jumped upon and eaten by the pieman. Eventually, the pieman himself fell asleep, gripping his saw. The others agreed they had to save themselves from this evil and that the pieman was the devil himself. The only chance was to scatter. The one man left with boots would go back to the logging crew and send for help. The other two, whose feet were badly sliced up from bushwhacking, would swim across the river to the rocky island they had seen from the riverbank the day before. They would hide out there from the pieman until help came."

"Convict Rock?" I ask.

Colin nods. "So you know the rest. No help came. The two men starved, too scared of the pieman and his handsaw to leave Convict Rock. The man with the boots made it back to the logging crew and the law eventually caught the pieman. He became infamous."

"But how did they know the other two died?" I asked. "Maybe they got away after all."

"That's the haunted part of the story. From the riverbank, for weeks and months afterward, people reported seeing the convicts waving from Convict Rock. Waving for help. But every time someone went over to look, no one was there. Eventually they found the skeletons of the two, curled up in a hollow together." He looks to the outline of the island. "But the sightings of one or both of them waving for help still went on. For years. That's how Convict Rock got its curse, or to be accurate, the superstition, the rumor, that it is haunted."

"Isn't this river called the Pieman River?" I ask.

"Affirmative," says Colin. "After Pieman the cannibal."

I can't help but shiver. What exactly have I done, asking to go to a haunted rock in the middle of a river named after a cannibal?

21

Moonlight Concert

Reeds poke up from the water, waving like wands, as the afternoon sunlight dances on the river. We're back in the skiff, but Uncle Ruff is now steering the boat and we're on our way to Convict Rock.

As we glide along the water, I think of the story Colin told me about the pieman and Convict Rock being haunted. Also, what Old Stevie had said about the place—that the tigers become ghosts there. But this is our last hope—for Ellie to still be on the rocky island, and to lure her out. I clutch my violin to my chest and feel the familiar nerves begin to build in my stomach. The plan to coax Ellie from hiding also means I have to play in front of Colin and Uncle Ruff.

Uncle Ruff steers us to a side of Convict Rock that isn't visible from the camp. We come around to an area with a gap in the low cliffs and a narrow area of flat sand.

"This is the only spot where we can beach the skiff," Uncle Ruff says. It takes quite a bit of maneuvering on Uncle Ruff's part to nose the small boat onto the narrow landing without crashing into the rock face. He jumps out first, stepping thigh high into the river. Colin throws him the rope and Uncle Ruff drags the boat higher up the riverbank, where the water is more shallow.

"Jump over," he calls to us. "This is as close as we're gonna get."

I look over the side of the boat realizing I'm going to have to get wet. I hand Colin my violin case and gingerly step over the side of the boat. The water is immediately icy through my runners and seeps into my socks, up to my ankles. I jump the few yards to the sandy shore and shake off my feet.

"The water is freezing!" I say.

"Huh!" says Ruff with a chuckle. "And that coming from a Canadian, no less."

Colin throws our gear from the skiff onto the bank before nimbly jumping out himself. He barely gets wet. Then the two of them tie up the skiff, anchoring it to a dead tree stump.

"Make sure she's tied up good and tight," says Ruff. "Otherwise we're swimming back." He gives me a wink. "Canadian polar bear style."

It's late afternoon, just before dusk. I grip my violin case and check that the backpack I'm carrying didn't get wet. We packed provisions to stay the night if necessary. I have a thermos of hot tomato soup, ham sandwiches, and extra socks that Uncle Ruff told me to bring, thank goodness, and a rain jacket. We also have a tent, sleeping bags, and thin sleeping mats.

"Come on," says Uncle Ruff after I've put on my dry socks. "I'll show you around before it gets dark."

The island is exactly as it appears from the camp. It's a long narrow rock, pocketed with many caves, some higher than eye level, others half buried below the sand line. We spend the last of the sunlight walking and climbing the rocky outcrop. Flat ground is rare. In a few places, low scrub clings to the sandy soil. A copse of trees juts out between the cliffs, their thick roots snaking down the rock face into the river.

As we scamper over Convict Rock my heart sinks further and further. The Rock feels totally and completely barren. It's impossible to imagine any living soul on it. I come to understand how unlikely it is that Ellie is here.

"If she's here," says Uncle Ruff, reading my thoughts, "she's holed up in an underground den." He points to low gaps at the base of the Rock, barely recognizable as cave entrances.

"Or she's just a ghost like the convicts," I say. "Which hollow did they find the convict bones in?" I ask.

"Bones?" says Uncle Ruff, flapping his hand in the air. "That's just an old wives' tale. Don't be giving any thought to it."

Colin and I exchange glances. We know he's just saying that so we don't get spooked.

"Come on, let's set up our camp," says Uncle Ruff. "It'll be dark soon."

Uncle Ruff chooses a mildly sloped area in sight of where

he had pointed out the low cave openings. He sets up the tent. It's hard going to hammer the tent pegs into the rough, dry ground. Colin meanwhile does an inventory of the food, water, sleeping bags, and mats. He arranges everything in a neat and orderly way.

"Once it gets dark, we'll want to know where everything is," he explains.

"Yep," agrees Uncle Ruff. "Once the sun goes down, it's gonna get chilly and dark pretty quick. We have a torch," he says holding up a flashlight, "but I only want to use it if we really need it."

"Can't we build a fire?" I ask.

"Nope," says Uncle Ruff. "We're here to catch a very shy creature. Torchlight and fire will keep her away, for sure." He pulls a grocery bag from his backpack and gives it a shake. "Roadkill. Wallaby and wombat mostly. I collect the hearts and innards, then freeze them. I thawed these out this morning. Should be good bait." He looks at me and smiles. "Hearts and violin, what could be more irresistible to a tiger?"

Colin and I peer into the plastic bag. I can't help but hold my nose. "Ew," I say. "Gross."

"Not if you're a tiger," says Uncle Ruff.

"Where will you set the bait?" asks Colin. "What's the plan?"

"I reckon I'll put the meat over there, by those bushes, halfway between the caves and Lou. If Ellie is attracted to the music, or the food, or both, she'll have cover in the bushes to eat and she'll feel safe." He gestures to Colin. "You and me, we'll hide on that low ridge behind the bushes with the net."

"And the lasso," Colin adds.

Uncle Ruff nods. "If Ellie comes out and sits still long enough, you can try and pin her with the lasso while I throw the net." He eyeballs us. "We have to be very, very gentle. Tigers are extremely timid. Remember, they have been known to faint, even die, from shock." He pauses. "If we do see her, there is nothing to be afraid of. Tigers are not aggressive animals. She will be curious and hungry, that's all. No sudden movements, no screaming. In fact, from now on, we talk softly. Once we have her safely, I have a tranquilizer to administer so she doesn't go into shock."

"And then what?" I ask.

Uncle Ruff taps his backpack. "I have a walkie-talkie here to radio Mel. She'll come in a bigger boat with the Elders. They know where to take her to safety."

Colin nods along while my stomach flips. I'm starting to feel like I'm in a spy movie.

"But first, you play," says Uncle Ruff to me. "If our hunch is right, she'll come out to see if it's other tigers. Then hopefully she'll go for the food." Uncle Ruff dusts off a boulder a few yards from the tent. "Here, this is a good spot for you to sit, Lou."

The light is dimming. Convict Rock and the sky have taken on a mauve hue.

"The magic hour," says Uncle Ruff noting the dusk. "Let's give this a shot, eh? It's now or never." He looks at me. "Just play like you usually do. No need for anything fancy. Remember, there's no bad notes. We're not sure what key might mimic the tiger's vocalization."

The three of us stack our palms silently on top of one another's, musketeer style.

"Okay. Let's go, mate," Uncle Ruff says to Colin. They gather up their gear for the ridge. Uncle Ruff puts his hand on my shoulder as he leaves. "Are you okay?" he asks.

I nod silently and sit with my violin case resting on my knees. My hands tremble as I open it.

"You could imagine that you are alone," Colin tells me as Uncle Ruff goes to drop the bait in the bushes. "Then you might not be affected by your performance anxiety."

Colin's acknowledgment of my anxiety is oddly comforting. I do exactly what he suggests. I close my eyes and pretend I'm alone on Convict Rock. It's easy to imagine. Even when I open my eyes again, all I see are the shadowy caves and the now-darkened sky. Colin and Uncle Ruff are hidden on the low ridge behind the bushes.

My hands are still shaking and my heart is fluttering as I warm up with the usual musical scales, but I close my eyes again and the nerves begin to ebb away. Just me and the ghosts. Besides, Colin and Uncle Ruff are not judging me, I tell myself. And Uncle Ruff, with his tone-deaf ear, he probably can't tell the difference between scales and Vivaldi. The thought makes me smile. I begin to relax and start to play the piece I've been practicing, one of Bach's adagio sonatas in G Minor. The notes drift freely into the chilly night air.

I'm not sure how long I've been playing when I feel Uncle Ruff touch my shoulder.

"Let's take a dinner break, kid," he says. "Nice music," he adds.

"Thanks. Any sign of Ellie?" I ask.

Uncle Ruff shakes his head. "Come on," he says, "let's get some tucker."

The three of us squeeze into the tent and I open the thermos with the tomato soup. It's no longer hot, but warm enough. Uncle Ruff shines the flashlight so I don't spill the soup as I pour out three cups. Colin passes around the ham sandwiches.

"Did you see anything at all?" I ask them as we eat our dinner in the dark tent. Their silence tells me all I need to know.

"We'll give it another go," says Uncle Ruff quietly after a while, but he can't hide the disappointment in his voice.

Once the soup and sandwiches are finished, we crawl out of the tent. The iridescent glow of the moon startles me. It's so bright now, like a giant luminous orb. Stars are scattered across the dark suede sky, glittering like jewels. I find the pointer stars, Alpha and Beta Centauri, then easily locate the Southern Cross crux. I point to the constellation and smile at Colin.

"I know exactly where I am," I tell him.

Uncle Ruff rushes over. "We're not the only ones who've had dinner," he says. "The bait is gone."

I grip Colin's arm in an excited panic.

"Quick!" says Uncle Ruff. "Let's get back to our places. I've put more bait down." He turns to me. "Your time to shine," he says, not realizing the phrase strikes panic in me. They both disappear again behind the ridge.

I sit down on the boulder with my violin. Maybe it's excitement, or nerves, or anxiety—I'm not sure if I can tell the difference—but I'm suddenly, stupidly, horribly self-conscious.

The stakes are higher now. I start to feel myself freeze. *Stop it*, I warn myself. *Stop being dumb. Just play. This is our last chance, Ellie is here somewhere, just play, don't let everyone down! You're being stupid!*

The more I talk to myself like this, the more my spine tenses and my arms stiffen.

Breathe. Close your eyes, I say instead. *Just like before, just like Colin told you.*

I sit this way for a while. I think about Ellie, all alone here, how scared she must be, probably much more scared than I am. Then I hear it. Faint piano music. Somewhere along the river, someone is playing the piano. And they're playing "Waltzing Matilda," just like Eleanor used to do. Hearing the familiar song eases my panic. Of course this is the song I have to play. *This is your concert, Ellie*, I tell her. *This is for you.* Slowly, slowly my arms loosen and the panic subsides. *Come on out, Ellie*, I tell her. *It's only me. We won't hurt you. You can trust us.* I start to play "Waltzing Matilda" by ear like I had done in the bush.

I finish the bush ballad and open my eyes.

I open my eyes just in time to see her.

Ellie is sitting a few yards from me. Moonglow reflects in the dark pools of her eyes. She stands and moves toward me with the grace and beauty of a creature that has walked the earth for tens of thousands of years. I am transfixed by her movement and by her large eyes, holding my gaze.

This all happens in an instant, before she is gone.

22

Ghost Piano

Ellie disappears into Ruff's burlap net.

"Torch!" I hear Ruff say, and a beam of light appears. Colin is holding the flashlight. Ruff holds the burlap netting over Ellie, but she does not appear to be struggling. He pulls a syringe out of his jacket and releases it into a part of her leg that is free. "It's okay, girl," I hear him croon. "It'll all be over soon." He holds the shape in the net firmly, continuing to talk softly to her. Colin and I are speechless. How can we speak? There are no words.

We crouch closer to Uncle Ruff as he eases off the burlap net. Ellie's head lolls as he lays her gently on the ground. She is asleep, sedated. "Is she okay?" I ask. Uncle Ruff pulls out a stethoscope and listens to her heart. "She's okay," he says. "But we haven't got much time." He looks to Colin. "Radio your mum, tell her to come quickly." Colin stumbles to the tent to find Uncle Ruff's backpack with the walkie-talkie.

"You did great, Lou," Uncle Ruff says to me.

"Can I touch her?" I ask.

"It's better you don't," says Uncle Ruff. "The less human scent on her the better. She'll need to find her pack soon. We don't want anything putting them off." He holds the flashlight so I can see her. "Take a good look though," he says. "I'm pretty sure this'll be the first and last time you ever see her."

In the beam of light, I study her tawny coat and dark markings. I count sixteen stripes running horizontally across her back. Her tail is long and stiff, almost like a kangaroo's, and I can just make out the opening of a pouch under her tail. Her legs look powerful, as does her jaw. Her snout is long and narrow, her ears pointed but also roundish. She looks to be about the size of a Doberman, but her legs are shorter.

"She is gorgeous," I say, spellbound.

"That she is," agrees Ruff. "She looks underweight. My guess is, with this sudden drop in temperature, the river became too cold for her to swim over to hunt. She's been stuck here without food. Your hunch was right on the money."

Colin rejoins us. "Mum will be here as soon as she can," he says breathlessly. "With the Elders."

"Okay, thanks mate. Good job," Uncle Ruff says to Colin. "Listen to me now, you two," he adds. "I know you want to stay, but you can't. Colin, you get the skiff and take Lou back to camp. Wait for us there."

Uncle Ruff sees us about to protest and puts his fingers to his lips.

"It has to be this way, trust me. You both need to go before Mel and the Elders get here. The fewer people involved the better."

We are disappointed but don't want to risk anything going wrong with the plan to get Ellie to safety.

"It was incredible," Colin says to me. "She was drawn to you like a magnet."

"It's true," says Uncle Ruff. "She seemed totally mesmerized by your playing the second time."

"I didn't even think I was going to be able to play," I tell them. "Until I heard the piano. You must have heard it too? Someone was playing 'Waltzing Matilda.'"

Both Uncle Ruff and Colin look confused. "All I heard was you playing 'Waltzing Matilda' on your violin," says Colin. "There's no other camps anywhere close to here. Nowhere that any other music could have been coming from."

"But I definitely heard it," I insist. "A piano. Someone playing 'Waltzing Matilda.'"

"The wind on the Rock can play tricks," is all Uncle Ruff says on the matter. "Come on now, time to get going. Off you go." He stands. "Be careful on the water. Wear your life jackets. Colin, use the motor on the skiff and go straight across the river to the camp. You'll be able to see the camp lights. Lou, keep the torch on the water."

We do as Uncle Ruff tells us. I look at Ellie one last time, committing the image of her slender beauty to my memory forever. We travel back in the skiff in mutual, companionable silence. I hold the flashlight, although we hardly need it because the river is bathed in moonlight. I can see our breath in the cold, clean air.

As we motor along, I can't help but wonder again about the piano. Was it my imagination and the wind playing tricks, like Uncle Ruff said? I guess I'll never know. What I do know is I feel a strong connection to my great-grandmother now, one that I could never have imagined possible.

Colin and I stay up the rest of the night, warm by the woodstove in Uncle Ruff's cabin, playing with Waltz and Matilda—who, being nocturnal, are full of beans.

"We met one of your distant cousins today," I tell Waltz as he scrambles up my shoulder and tries to climb my hair. I laugh as he tickles my ear with his wet nose.

Even Colin, who is usually a stickler for routine, doesn't want to go to bed. Going to sleep would break the spell. We don't want to let the magic slip away. And *magical* is the only way to describe it. Our magical, mysterious, and extraordinary night on Convict Rock.

As we sit watching the fire, juggling the devil joeys, I ask Colin to describe his version of the events from behind the ridge.

"It was pitch-black behind the ridge," he says. "Except for the moonlight. That's how we saw her, the moonlight cast a shadow as she came out of her den. Then she sat and listened to your music. We were watching her watch you. To be accurate, it was approximately ten seconds. And then she began to creep closer to you. That's when Ruff threw the net. I didn't have time to use the lasso, unfortunately." Colin stops and thinks for a few minutes. "It was like...it almost looked like...she knew you."

23

Cicero

With the first songbirds at dawn, we hear tires crunching up the gravel road to the camp. Colin and I go to the window and see Mel and Uncle Ruff pull up in Mel's SUV. I put the kettle on to make tea and Colin pulls a quiche from the oven. He spent the wee hours preparing breakfast for us.

In the early light I notice a heavy fog has settled in. It hugs the forest canopy, obscuring the treetops. It gives the camp a ghostly appearance, which is fitting enough, because before long it will all be gone.

The grown-ups come into the cabin and we all hug one another. It's the first time I've felt Uncle Ruff's big arms around me.

"Ellie is safe," says Mel. "And hopefully with other tigers now." She pats our backs. "You two did an amazing thing. Well done."

Colin and I smile. "Come and eat," I say. "Look what Colin made."

We sit and have our breakfast together, happy, relieved, but sad too, knowing our next step is to clear out of the camp. The plan is for us to take the devil joeys and our things to the Eco Lodge today. Uncle Ruff doesn't want to be here when the construction crew inevitably turn up.

"I'm going to take a walk," I say once the breakfast dishes are done. "I won't be long."

The dawn fog has lifted to reveal a piercingly blue sky. The air is so clean, the sun so bright, it's like I'm inside a digital image. I read somewhere that the Tasmanian forest has the cleanest air on the planet and I can believe it. Melancholy grows at the thought of leaving, even worse to imagine this place not being here one day.

I walk slowly under the groves of blue gums. The canopy is dotted with gaps where fallen giant trees have given way, crashing to the forest floor, allowing the smaller trees to flourish. Spiderwebs in the fern fronds catch the sunlight, illuminating the dew clinging to the webs.

I reach the mossy log and sit down after checking for snakes. For once, I don't have my violin. I want to hear the music of the forest instead. I sit and listen to the currawongs sing their Vivaldi chorus and the rhythmic swish and sway of the towering giants above me. I close my eyes, breathe in the lemon myrtle, and listen carefully. I want to imprint it all in my memory forever.

When I get back to the camp, Mel and Colin have started to pack things into the SUV. I go into the cabin; Uncle Ruff is throwing items into garbage bags. I can see that he has packed boxes with Eleanor's journal, his laptop, and books.

"Here it is," I hear him say. He comes to the kitchen holding a cloth bag.

"What is it?" I ask.

"It's Eleanor's," he says, handing me a small pillow with cross-stitching. "She stitched it when she was young. Girls did that kind of thing in those days."

Cross-stitched on the pillow are the words:

> *Art is born*
> *of the observation*
> *and investigation*
> *of nature.*

"It's a quote by Cicero. He was a Roman philosopher. Eleanor really believed it too. That all truly meaningful pursuits are inspired by observing nature." He pauses. "Anyway, I wanted you to give it to your mum. Well, it's for all of you. You and Sophie too. So you all have something of Eleanor's. There's so little left since the fire."

I hug the pillow gently. "It's perfect," I say. "Thank you."

"No, Lou, thank *you*," he says. "I've gotta admit that when your mum told me she wanted to send you here, I wasn't too happy about it. There was so much going on. With Piggy and the construction. It just seemed, well, a bad time. But I was wrong. You've been amazing. Truly. We never would have saved Ellie without you. Our very own tiger whisperer. Eleanor would have been impressed." He ruffles my hair. "All that and you outsmarted the bunyips too."

We both laugh, remembering.

"That's because Canadians are actually tougher than Australians," I tease.

"Oh, hey now!" he says. "Them's fightin' words." He looks at me sideways. "But maybe I need to come over there to check it out for myself, eh?"

"You'll come to visit us in Toronto?" I ask hopefully.

"Seems like a good time to do some traveling," he says. "I've been holed up here for too long. There's a whole world out there I need to explore." He gives me a wink. "Not to mention a couple of nieces and a sister that I have to check up on."

We walk outside to the riverbank and sit together on the smooth rocks. We look out over the sparkling water to the outline of Convict Rock. I'm still holding Eleanor's cross-stitch pillow.

"Do you think Ellie will make it?" I ask.

"She was in pretty good shape, all things considered," he answers. "Whatever prevented her from leaving with the pack, it wasn't evident. I couldn't find any obvious injuries or breaks."

"And what about the other tigers, will they all survive?" I ask. "How will we know?"

"We won't. But we know we've done our best to give them a chance." Uncle Ruff throws a pebble into the river. "If the tigers are left alone, and their habitat is left alone, they might have a chance to repopulate." He looks at me. "It's likely there are more packs on the island. There's still a lot of sightings in the northeast of Tasmania as well." We watch as his pebble skips over the water. "Humans. We think we know everything. The truth is, we know very little when it comes to the natural world. Except how to take what we want from it." He sighs deeply. "But it's happened before, you know. Species that are believed to be extinct show up again."

"Really?" I say.

"Really," he says. "You should read some of your dad's articles sometime."

I hang my head with a smile. He's right.

"There's a pocket-sized carnivorous marsupial called the crest-tailed mulgara," Ruff says. "Actually, a relative of the Tasmanian devil and the tiger, that was thought to be extinct in the state of New South Wales for over a hundred years. Then recently, a young crest-tailed mulgara was found in the Stuart National Park there. And a pygmy tarsier," he goes on. "A nocturnal primate, native to Sulawesi, Indonesia, was believed extinct for eighty years before being rediscovered by an Indonesian scientist in 2000. He accidentally caught it in a rat trap." He skips another pebble. "So who knows. Maybe if humans can keep out of their way long enough, and stop destroying their habitat, the tigers will make their big comeback."

"I hope so," I say.

"Me too, kid."

We sit together in silence listening to the gentle rush of the water until Uncle Ruff points out a flock of black swans. "Look there," he says. "Black swans."

We watch as the majestic black swans make their leisurely progress downriver.

The rest of the day is spent packing the cars and the skiff with everything worth saving. By late afternoon we're ready to leave. Colin and I will go upriver to the Eco Lodge in the skiff while Mel and Ruff will drive with the joeys.

"I'm not into mushy goodbyes," Uncle Ruff warns us. "I'll see youse back at the Eco Lodge."

As we wave at Uncle Ruff's jeep and watch it bump down the driveway, I notice that he left a cascade of pom-pom shaped golden wattle flowers on Piggy's grave.

24

The Black Swan Theory

At the Eco Lodge, a few days before my flight home to Toronto, Uncle Ruff says it's time to take Waltz and Matilda to the devil sanctuary in Cradle Mountain. It's on the way to Launceston where I'll catch my flight. He says he wants to show me more of the island before I go home, but I suspect he can't bear to be in the Tarkine when the demolition begins. Anyway, the task of giving up Waltz and Matilda is too much to do alone.

Mel has learned that the construction crew will start, as planned, in a few days. Colin will join our sightseeing trip too. It will be his last hurrah before going back to school, Mel tells us.

I'm grateful to have access to a computer at the Eco Lodge

so I can e-mail my family about everything that's happened. I've missed them. But strangely, even though I haven't seen or spoken to them for weeks, I feel closer to all of them.

Saying goodbye to Mel is harder than I imagined.

She kisses my cheek. "Your mum is so proud of you, you know," she says, hugging me tightly. "And thank you," she whispers in my ear. "I want to tell you something else," she adds, cupping my face in her hands. "Following your passion takes hard work, but more important, it takes courage. I see that in you. Keep going. Don't give up."

My throat tightens. "Thank you," I manage to say to her finally. "I won't. I promise."

After spending so much time deep in the rain forest, once we get out on the road, I'm surprised to notice how diverse the landscape is as we make our way to Cradle Mountain. We pass through sweeping highlands, alpine vistas, and button grasslands.

"Is this the same road I took on the bus?" I ask Uncle Ruff.

"Yep," he says. "One and the same."

"Amazing. I can't believe I didn't notice how stunning the scenery was the first time."

"You probably had other things on your mind," says Uncle Ruff.

It's true, I did. I put my hand on my violin case, safely tucked on the seat next to me.

Waltz and Matilda are traveling in a small dog crate at my feet. They've slept most of the way but I can hear them begin to squeak. I open the crate and take Waltz out and stroke him on my lap. "Before long you're going to be a real tough guy," I tell him. "But you'll always be sweet to me."

Waltz gnaws on my thumb. I can feel the nubs of his growing teeth. Those teeth, when Waltz is fully grown, will kill and devour the entire carcass of his prey, and his cute squeaks will become the devil's signature growl. Sounds which I'm astonished to hear when we pull up at the devil sanctuary. As soon as we step out of the car, we hear disconcertingly loud screeching and growling. I hold Waltz close to my chest.

"Ah, good ol' devil chitchat," says Uncle Ruff. "Must be feeding time."

"Best keep them in the crate now," he tells me. I reluctantly put Waltz back in the crate as a small crowd of people greet us from the sanctuary. There's a lot of back-slapping and "G'day mates!" all around. Uncle Ruff seems very popular.

"He knows some of them from veterinary school," Colin informs me. "And the others from when he volunteered here when he was young."

As Uncle Ruff talks with his friends, Colin and I say goodbye to Waltz and Matilda. They squeak and sniff at our fingers between the bars of the crate.

"Have a good life," Colin says to them. "Stay healthy."

"Be good devils," I tell them.

"Come on." Uncle Ruff motions to us. "Let's take these guys to the nursery."

Our hearts lift seeing all the devil joeys running around in the nursery.

"So many friends for Waltz and Matilda," says Colin hopefully.

"Don't worry about all the noisy growling," one of the sanctuary rangers tells us. "It's just a lot of big-boy chitchat during mealtimes. These babies are going to be just fine here. This is where they should be. We can assure that they won't contract the facial disease that's rampant among the wild population right now. They'll grow to be big and healthy and grumpy like all their new friends here."

I smile, watching a dozen joeys scamper, claw, and run over one another in a large grassy enclosure. Some tumble and chew on each other in pretend fights. The caretakers are so loving and enthusiastic it's hard to feel too sad. A ranger takes the crate. "We'll need to do some tests before releasing them into the nursery population. Time to say goodbye."

And just like that, our charges are gone.

We stay a little while longer, watching the nursery joeys chase after a ranger in what looks like a crazy-cute devil version of follow the leader, until Uncle Ruff says we'd better get back on the road.

Our continuing journey is tinged with beauty and melancholy. Cradle Mountain is so beautiful. We spend a few days hiking to various lookout points, where we gaze at the layered mountain ranges, crystal lakes, and the endless blue haze of eucalypts. But we're also sad and homesick for the ramshackle camp in the Tarkine. We miss our devil babies and we're heartsick for Convict Rock. We're doing our best not to picture the camp being bulldozed and Convict Rock dynamited.

Our final days and hours together go by too quickly. Before we know it, Uncle Ruff's jeep is pulling up at Launceston airport and I am about to begin the long journey home to Toronto. Uncle Ruff carries my duffel bag to the departure terminal. Colin trails behind. He's trying to delay my leaving by walking slowly. I check in at the airline counter and we walk together to the security gate. An airline agent is there to meet me because I'm traveling as an unaccompanied minor.

"This is it, kid," says Uncle Ruff. "You know I don't do mushy goodbyes."

"I know," I say.

"Come here then," he says, enveloping me in his bear hug. I feel his scratchy beard graze my cheek.

"Visit soon," I tell him.

"You can count on it," he says.

Colin hangs back. He watches me from the corners of his large owl eyes. He is tapping.

"Do you have your phone?" I ask him.

Colin pulls his phone from his pocket and holds it up to take my photo.

"No. Wait," I say, gesturing for him to stand next to me. I take the phone and angle it above our heads to take a selfie. I hand the phone back to him.

"Call that one *Friends*," I say. We laugh, remembering our day in the bush. "I'm going to hug you now," I tell him, "and I want you to hug me back."

Colin leans in to me and we say we'll always be there for each other. We agree to stay in touch, and to text and call each other all the time, especially on the hard days.

"You're the smartest and kindest person I've ever met," I tell him. "I'm proud to call you my friend."

"Time to go, miss," says the airline agent.

"Take good care of her," Uncle Ruff tells her. "She's a special one."

"To be accurate," says Colin to the airline agent, wiping tears from his cheeks, "she's my best friend."

On our last day by the river, Uncle Ruff had told me about the black swan theory. Back in old England, the phrase "black swan" was used as a metaphor for something that was impossible. It was a phrase used in the same way that we say "if pigs could fly." When explorers saw the wild black swans in Australia for the first time, the phrase changed. It came to mean something that was once *thought* to be impossible, but actually proven to be possible.

I'm back in Toronto now but I still have black swans on my mind.

And tigers.

The day of my audition for the youth orchestra has arrived. I've taken my seat in the auditorium and I've let the judges know that I have anxiety and that I need a few moments to practice the breathing method that can help me. I note with surprise that my therapist is right: the jury members are not scandalized by my confession.

I've been seeing a therapist since I returned from Tasmania and told my family about my anxiety. They were grateful that I was finally able to talk to them about what had been troubling me. They've all been incredibly supportive. I've also been doing cognitive behavioral therapy, practicing breathing methods for when panic grips me.

"Take your time," is all the audition judges say now.

The judges talk casually among themselves while I use the minutes on my breathing exercises, just like Mom and I have been doing together in the car. Mom is waiting for me outside the audition room. It gives me huge comfort to know she is close by, rooting for me. I know Colin is doing the same for me on the other side of the world. His latest text was brimming with news about making friends in a club at his school where they play a strategy card game called *Magic: The Gathering*.

Remember, you are brave, he reminded me. *You keep trying.*

I breathe out his words with each exhale.

I close my eyes.

I see Ellie emerging from the shadows to sit gracefully and patiently for her music. She blinks her onyx eyes in the moonlight, waiting. I hear the Tasmanian currawong birds singing their Vivaldi chorus and I feel the blue gums swaying high above me in perfect rhythm.

"Before I play the required classical pieces, I'd like to perform a folk ballad. It's called 'Waltzing Matilda,'" I tell the judges. "I learned it this summer in the Tasmanian rain forest." I pause.

"My great-grandmother taught it to me."

The judges nod encouragingly and motion for me to begin.

Once again, just as I did on Convict Rock, I hear Eleanor's piano.

I lift my bow, and together we begin to play.

Epilogue

I received mail from Uncle Ruff today. I opened the envelope eagerly, expecting a letter, but what I found inside was a newspaper clipping recounting a recent local event:

TASMANIAN CHRONICLE

Danish Hiker Says "Striped" Protectors Kept Him From Losing Hope During His 7-Day Ordeal!

After a tense, weeklong search-and-rescue effort in Tasmania's northwest, a Danish hiker has miraculously been found alive and well.

Despite being warned repeatedly of the dangers by local rangers, twenty-five-year-old Jens Andersen set out on a solo hiking expedition in the remote northwestern Tarkine wilderness. His location was many kilometres from the better-known tourist trails of the area. When the adventurer failed to return to his hostel on the appointed day, the owners of the backpacker accommodations alerted authorities. A costly rescue mission was launched to find Andersen who, while being an experienced survivalist and outdoorsman, is unfamiliar with the rugged terrain.

The search-and-rescue mission began looking for Andersen on foot, later deploying a helicopter to further comb the near-impenetrable area. Andersen was found on the seventh day with a broken ankle at the bottom of a ravine, having fallen from the cliff top a week prior. He was dehydrated, but alive. Luckily, he had carried a backpack with food and water rations. He was also able to collect rainwater to drink.

After he was rescued, the survivor recounted a fantastical story of being kept company by a pair of "striped dogs":

"On the first few nights stuck in the ravine I saw the silhouette of a wild doglike creature with a striped back and a long, powerful jaw. I was initially frightened, thinking the creature planned to attack. But night after night it appeared on the ridge, just to observe. Perhaps it was waiting for me to die, I thought. But then after I spent many days stuck there, a second, smaller striped dog joined the first. This one came closer than its mate, especially if I was singing. To keep up my spirits and help the boredom I sang every song I could think of. The smaller one seemed to like listening to the music. I don't know what I would have done without their silent, protective company. Without them I would have felt totally and absolutely alone. They watched over me and kept me from losing hope."

While the description of the animals sounds uncannily like that of the thylacine, or Tasmanian tiger as it is popularly known, authorities dismissed the story, stating the individual was delirious from dehydration and was likely experiencing hallucinations. A local ranger who says he is often alerted to supposed sightings of the tiger stated:

"Tasmanian tigers are extinct and have been since 1936. No evidence has been found here or anywhere else on the island to prove otherwise. Usually an overactive imagination sees a devil or a wild dog and they think it's a tiger. It's not. If tigers still existed here, we would have found evidence, remains, scat, or footprints. Nothing has been found for decades. The tiger is extinct. People just refuse to accept it."

Jens Andersen is currently recovering from his injuries in the North West Regional Hospital and plans to return to Copenhagen once the medical team approves his discharge. Andersen sketched a likeness of his striped wilderness companions, which accompanies this article. The reader can judge the resemblance for themselves. But one thing is certain, the mystery of whether the Tasmanian tiger still exists remains alive and well.

Andersen's sketch of his striped wilderness companions

At the end of the article, Uncle Ruff had written:

G'day, Lou,
Thought you'd like to see
what Ellie's been up to.
Love, Uncle Ruff

Tasmanian Tiger

The Tasmanian tiger, known to science as the thylacine, was the world's largest carnivorous marsupial. Historically, the tiger was widespread across Australia before becoming extinct on the mainland around 3,000 years ago. The Tasmanian tiger population became isolated from the mainland by rising sea levels around 14,000 years ago.

A cash bounty offered for dead tigers was started in Tasmania in the 1800s in response to a perceived threat to the European settlers' farm livestock. By 1914 concerns were being raised for the tiger's survival, but all too late. The last captive tiger, known as Benjamin, died in Hobart Zoo on September 7, 1936, and the species was declared officially extinct in 1986. **Threatened Species Day** is now held each year on September 7 to commemorate the anniversary of Benjamin's death and to reflect on how we can protect threatened species in the future.

In 1914, Tasmanian biologist **Professor T.T. Flynn** (father of the 1930s–'50s Hollywood actor Errol Flynn) proposed an island sanctuary be established to protect the species. Sadly, it was never acted upon for the tigers, but today **Maria Island** is a national park that provides sanctuary for the endangered Tasmanian devil, along with many other native Australian birds and marsupials. Maria Island has been described as Tasmania's Noah's Ark.

The loss of a species through extinction is without doubt an environmentally tragic event. Worse still when it seems, as in the tiger's case, to have been caused by senseless hunting.

Music for Tigers is a work of fiction, but could the Tasmanian tiger still exist? Could it reappear as other extinct species have done? While there has been no authenticated evidence of its existence since 1936, sightings continue, with many staunch believers remaining certain that the species, while elusive, continues to exist today.

To learn more about the setting of the story, the **Tasmanian Tarkine/takayna** and the campaign to have the area recognized as a National Park and World Heritage Area, please visit:

**Bob Brown Foundation, Action for Earth:
www.bobbrown.org.au.**

Tasmania's Convict History

Tasmania is an island state of Australia, separated from the mainland by 150 miles of rough water called the Bass Strait. It is a remote area of the world, known for its vast and rugged wilderness, and as the gateway to Antarctica. These days it is easy to reach Tasmania by airplane and ferry; however, back in the early 1800s, it could take up to eight months for ships to reach Van Diemen's Land, as it was known then. Its isolation was seen by British settlers as an ideal location for a convict colony. For the first fifty years of its settlement it was used for that purpose, with 76,000 convicts sent there from all over the British Empire. The average sentence for prisoners, usually petty thieves, was seven years in what was described as "the end of the world."

The escaped convict story that appears on page 150 is fictional; however it is loosely based on true characters. The real pieman was Thomas Kent from England, a pastry cook who was transported to Van Diemen's Land in 1816. In 1822 he escaped and was recaptured near the mouth of the river that now bears his nickname. A fellow convict, Irish-born Alexander Pearce, escaped from prison several times. During one of these escapes he allegedly became a cannibal, killing his companions one by one. He was hanged for murder in Hobart in 1824.

Species Extinction

Species extinction occurs when environmental factors or evolutionary problems cause a species to die out completely. The disappearance of species from earth is ongoing, and rates have varied over time. According to the Red List of the IUCN **(International Union of Conservation for Nature**) a quarter of mammals are at risk of extinction.

To some extent, extinction is natural. Changes to habitats and poor reproductive trends are among the factors that can make a species' death rate higher than its birth rate such that eventually none are left.

Humans also cause species to become extinct by hunting, overharvesting, introducing invasive species to the wild, polluting, and changing wetlands and forests to croplands and urban areas. Even the rapid growth of the human population is causing extinction by ruining natural habitats.

If you are interested in reading about species extinction and how we can help to prevent further loss of endangered animals and their habitat, here are some organizations where you can learn more.

- **WWF** is the world's leading independent conservation organization. Its global mission is to stop the degradation of the planet's natural environment and to build a future in which humans live in harmony with nature.

- **WWF—Australia** is a part of the WWF Global Network.

- **Global Wildlife Conservation's** mission is to conserve the diversity of life on earth, where all life has value and can flourish—plant, animal, and human.

- **International Union of Conservation of Nature's Red List:** Established in 1964, the International Union for Conservation of Nature's Red List of Threatened Species has evolved to become the world's most comprehensive information source on the global conservation status of animal, fungi and plant species.